Hurricane
Girl

Hurricane Girl

MARCY DERMANSKY

ALFRED A. KNOPF

NEW YORK

2022

THIS IS A BORZOI BOOK PUBLISHED BY ALFRED A. KNOPF

Copyright © 2022 by Marcy Dermansky

www.aaknopf.com

LIBRARY OF CONGRESS CATALOGING-IN-PUBLICATION DATA
Names: Dermansky, Marcy, 1969– author.
Title: Hurricane girl : a novel / Marcy Dermansky.
Description: First edition.
Identifiers: LCCN 2021009360
ISBN 9780593320884 (hardcover)
ISBN 9780593315354 (paperback)
ISBN 9780593320891 (ebook)
Classification: LCC PS3604.E7545 H87 2022
DDC 813/.6—DC23
LC record available at https://lccn.loc.gov/2021009360

Jacket design by Janet Hansen
Jacket illustration by Tyler Spangler

Manufactured in the United States of America
First Edition

Part
One

Allison Brody bought a beach house.

She was thirty-two years old.

Sick of everybody and everything.

All she wanted to do, more than anything, really, was swim.

The beach house was small. It was in North Carolina, in foreclosure. She had put cash down, emptying her accounts, everything that she had. She used money saved from waitressing, money saved from a small inheritance from her father when he died, almost a year ago. She had sold a script, too, and made some okay money from that. A solid chunk. It was a horror script. It would not necessarily make a good film, but a famous actress had agreed to star in it, and so there could be more money. More scripts. Success.

Allison had been seen as a movie producer's pretty younger girlfriend. She could have been known in her own right. Probably it had been stupid to leave Los Angeles just when her career started taking off and there were so many places to swim. The movie producer, for instance, had a beautiful swimming pool.

Maybe. Maybe leaving had been stupid.

Maybe Allison wanted to create art one day. After she swam. Maybe, one day, she would want to have a cat. The movie producer was allergic to cats.

Maybe she actually wanted to live alone, and certainly not with a man who hit her. It had happened only a few times, exactly three, but it also seemed possible that it could happen again, even though the movie producer had promised that it wouldn't.

She drove cross-country, doing the speed limit, buying coffees from Starbucks along the way.

And the beach house turned out to be perfect.

Two small bedrooms and a bathroom on the second floor with a view of the ocean. A front porch where Allison could drink her coffee and breathe in the ocean air.

Almost all Allison knew about North Carolina was from a long-ago vacation, and it was wonderful, her favorite childhood memory. The road trip had been insanely long. A caravan with another family. They had taken regimented bathroom stops. When she woke, she had been delivered to a house with an oval swimming pool and a view of the ocean. Allison remembered a large, pink dolphin float in the pool, with a cup holder built into it for drinks. All the parents got drunk every night and everyone laughed a lot and the kids were allowed to do whatever they wanted.

~~~~~

Allison had lived in her beach house for a week and a half when the hurricane warning came. Category Five. Orders to evacuate.

She spent a night in a motel.

She drank gin and tonics, her father's favorite drink, and watched the local news in her motel room.

Her father, she knew, would have told her to buy the beach house. He would have told her, not for the first time, about the beach house he did not buy, years ago, a decision he regretted to his death. Allison's mother had not wanted to spend the money. Take that risk.

Whereas Allison had bought the house. It would be okay. That was what she told herself.

And, in the end, in fact, the storm was reduced to Category Three and had turned north. Allison felt grateful to be spared. She got up, only slightly hungover, bought a coffee, and drove back to her house. Which was gone. She did find it, but in pieces strewn all over the yard. Wood beams and siding everywhere. The toilet, from the second floor, was upright in the same place, on the ground. The red couch was precisely where it had been, in the living room that no longer existed. The roof lay in the middle of the road. Strangely, the steps up to the now-absent porch were still intact.

When Allison first heard about the storm, she imagined she would weather it. But then the winds picked up and she realized she was afraid.

Her neighbor next door had nailed boards across his windows. Allison thought about asking him to help her. Allison also did not want help from men. She also did not like the look of her neighbor. He wore a baseball cap and had large muscles, wore sleeveless T-shirts that said USA.

"Bye, house," Allison said as she sank down on the front steps, clutching her cup of Dunkin' Donuts coffee. That was all she could find that morning on the drive from the motel. "I loved you."

Allison was not sure what to do.

She thought about sitting on the front steps, but probably that was not safe. She had spent so many good hours on the porch, imagining her future.

The house was insured, at least.

She was not a complete idiot.

"You are an idiot," Allison said out loud with a sigh.

Allison had a tendency to be unkind to herself.

In this case, it seemed warranted.

Her mother, always a worrier, had advised her against the move. Her friend Lori had also been against it. "You won't like it there," Lori had said. "The beach might be good, sure, but think about hurricane season. Republicans. White supremacists."

Allison had claimed not to be scared of such things.

"Well then you are an idiot," Lori had said.

Allison often wished that she had a best friend who was nicer to her. Often, it felt like not enough people were nice to her. Her next boyfriend, if nothing else, would be nice.

Allison stretched her arms out to the sky.

She was incredibly stiff, as if all of the tension of the day before was somehow stored in her body. She walked around the foundation of her house, taking pictures with her cell phone. There was one of her sneakers, blown on top of the neighbor's hedge. The hedges were still perfect. The neighbor's house did not look damaged. It was a brick house. Sturdy.

Allison's house, clearly, had not been particularly sturdy.

She had forgone any inspection. She had had to act fast. It was an auction, no time to be careful. Allison had worried, driving cross-country, that there would not even be a house, that she had participated in an elaborate Internet scam.

So the whole thing had not been a complete loss.

Allison's phone rang, but she did not answer it. It was her mother. The kind thing to do, of course, would have been to answer it. Allison had not even listened to the messages that had started coming in once the hurricane began.

She did not think that her mother would actually say *I told you so,* but somehow her not saying so would not take away the sting. Her mother *had* told her so.

Allison was homeless and she was broke.

It was wild how fast the tides could turn.

Part of her also knew that she was fine.

She would make more money. Find a more appropriate home. Allison could write another script. She could even go back to her movie producer boyfriend. She could go back to his beautiful house and swim in his beautiful pool. He had not wanted her to leave. She could get back into her car and do the trip in reverse, make time move backward. She could wait for her insurance money to come in.

Allison stared at the red couch. She had bought it new at IKEA. She had not even hung any art on the walls.

This was not so bad.

Even if it *felt* that bad.

And it did feel that bad.

~~~~~

*I*n her week and a half in the house, Allison had not met anyone. Had barely had a conversation. She had gone swimming every day, jumping waves, floating on her back. She had taken long walks on the beach. She had watched rabbits run from the bushes at the edge of her yard and then take cover. She had eaten turkey sandwiches for lunch and then sometimes turkey sandwiches for dinner.

Until the day of the hurricane, the weather had been perfect. Allison had an idea for a new screenplay, a TV show maybe, but she did not try to write it. She knew that when the time came, it would be there, waiting for her, inside her very good brain. She had time.

Somehow, she felt busy. Swimming every day. Taking walks. She would have time to write. She could wait for the rain, she told herself.

She had not considered that it would rain as hard as it did.

It did not seem fair that the houses on either side of Allison's were still standing. It made Allison think of the Three Little Pigs. She, of course, had gotten the house made of sticks. The neighbor in the baseball cap pulled into the driveway of the brick house next door.

"Tough luck," he called out to her, getting out of the car.

"Right?" she said.

"Let me know if you want to sell the land. I'd be happy to take it off your hands."

"What?" Allison asked.

So much for one moment of sympathy.

He handed her a business card.

"It would be foolhardy to rebuild, don't you think? I can pay you a good price."

Allison looked at the card. Jim Smith. That was really his name. She had the urge to ask him how he spelled it.

It did not seem like a particularly kind offer to buy her land. But it did not seem like a bad idea, either.

"I was supposed to buy it, but the realtor was a cunt."

Allison squinted at him. Jim Smith.

"She said she was going to email me the paperwork and then sold the property out from under me."

Allison could hear a voice in her head: her father, telling her to make a deal. Ask for more than it's worth. She could ask for a lot. She could seek out that same realtor, the one who clearly loathed him. Jim Smith. Allison was glad, at least, that he would no longer be her neighbor.

Allison shrugged. "This just happened," she said. "I don't know what I am going to do."

"Just think about it," her neighbor said. "And make sure you clean up this mess," he said. "It's an eyesore."

Allison said nothing. She watched Jim Smith head inside his house, close the front door.

Asshole.

Allison squeezed her eyes shut. She wanted her house back.

Anyway, it was not a complete disaster.

Allison had saved her clothes. Her laptop computer. Her

cell phone. Her expensive facial lotion. A favorite coffee mug she had bought more than ten years ago, taken with her from one home to the next. It was white, with a green fish painted on it. There were yellow strips above and below the fins. It was a random design. Allison loved this mug.

She had barely furnished the house. She had been planning on taking her time. She did not need, for instance, a kitchen table. She ate her turkey sandwiches sitting on her front porch. She had bought a couch. And look what had happened to that.

Anyway, she was fine. She still had her health. That was what people liked to say. She had her health.

～～～～

A van with a news station logo turned the corner.

A skinny man wearing a Panama shirt and cargo shorts waved at her, and then the van pulled over and he hopped out. He had skinny legs, wiry knees. Wire-rimmed glasses, sandy blond hair, a large bald spot. Allison realized she was staring at him. He had a video camera slung over his shoulder. He had to be a cameraman.

Allison still felt annoyed by her interaction with her neighbor. She wondered whether she had to talk to this cameraman. She did not want to talk to him. Usually, though, it was more awkward to be rude than to be polite.

"Is that your house?" the cameraman asked her. "Is that your roof on the street?"

Allison nodded.

Probably, she would have to talk.

"Would you mind giving an interview?"

A skinny blond woman also stepped out of the van. She was made-up, ready. She was wearing a short black skirt, a pink silk tank top. Clearly, they had been cruising the neighborhood, looking for something to shoot. Allison had watched that same woman on the news, in the motel, the night before. She had been wearing a bright yellow raincoat, holding an umbrella, warning people to take cover as tree branches flew by. She looked afraid, but gamely talked on. Tabitha Crosby, Allison remembered. Allison had been worried about her. Life was funny. Allison was glad Tabitha Crosby was okay, so she agreed.

Years from now, Allison decided, she would be able to watch her younger self standing in front of her ruined house. It was part of her story now. She was lucky, really, to have this chance to document her misfortune.

Allison looked down at her cut-off jean shorts. The white T-shirt she had slept in. She could certainly be dressed better for TV. For her mother's sake. For posterity.

She considered putting on lipstick, but that would seem strange considering what she was wearing. Allison's hair was pulled back into a messy ponytail, and she wanted to brush it but did not know how to ask for more time.

The cameraman had placed a big white light-shade thing on the sidewalk, then Tabitha Crosby, fresh and impossibly dewy in her silk tank top, reapplied *her* lipstick, and they were ready to go.

"Let's do this," Tabitha said.

Probably it made for better TV if Allison was a mess. Probably they wanted Allison to cry. The crazy thing was that once she was on camera, Allison felt tears well up in her eyes.

"No, I don't know what I am going to do next," she said slowly, thinking out loud. "I don't know where I will wake up tomorrow. This was my home. I spent all of my money on this house."

It sounded bad when she said the words out loud.

Allison had wanted this house to be her home.

"I am fine," she said. "I really am. I have my health."

"God bless," Tabitha Crosby said. It was strange to hear these words come out of a journalist's mouth.

Allison would never say that.

Allison did not have a chance to explain, on camera, that she did not believe in God.

God, if she considered it, seemed awfully cruel and violent, blowing people's houses down, washing out the coastline. Such a God, Allison was sure, would have to be a man, and not a particularly nice one.

Allison's friend Lori had warned her that she did not belong there. It turned out to be true. She didn't belong in a North Carolina beach town.

She certainly had not belonged in Los Angeles, and she had tried. Hot yoga and wax treatments and wearing tight clothes to film premieres had not worked out for her, either.

The interview ended, and Tabitha Crosby and the cameraman got back into their van and drove away.

It was amazing how angry Allison found herself at that moment, at Lori, who had done nothing but give Allison her opinion and be right.

~~~~~

Allison went to a local restaurant, sat at the bar, and ordered a cheeseburger and a draft beer. She drank the beer fast, waiting for her cheeseburger. It was only after she had finished the beer that she noticed the cameraman, two barstools away from her, also drinking a beer.

"Hurricane Girl," he said.

Allison nodded.

"That's me."

"Let me buy you the next round," he said.

The bartender came around and put the cheeseburger in front of Allison.

"I'll buy your burger, too. You did lose a house, after all. You deserve a free meal. How does that sound?"

"Sure," Allison said.

The logic made perfect sense to her.

"Can I join you?" he asked.

"Sure," she said.

She was not entirely sure, but she had drunk that first beer quickly and it would be awkward eating her dinner with an empty barstool between them. The cameraman did not order food for himself, only another drink. A whiskey this time. It looked good to her, but she was driving. The cameraman asked Allison if she wanted one and she shook her head no, because she was driving. She assumed he was, too, but it was not up to her to judge. Really, the world was full of drunk drivers. It was always safer to stay home, but Allison no longer had a home.

It seemed safe to assume that the cameraman was hitting on her. He was older, in his fifties, maybe, possibly older than that, his face wrinkled; he was not her type, but maybe that was not necessarily a terrible thing. If her house hadn't blown down, she might have been more likely to say no without even considering the offer.

A cheeseburger and a beer. Why not? A week and a half was a long time not to be around other people. What was the harm? Her house had already blown down. Crazy as it seemed, Allison had made an actual plan for her life. Now she had to start all over. She did not want to go back to the motel. She did not want to go back to her hometown, to New Jersey. She did not know where she was going to go next. She had made a list of places in her journal the night before, watching hurricane coverage on the news. She had made lists according to desirability: East Coast, West Coast, couches versus spare rooms. There was always, obviously, her mother's house. Her childhood bedroom, except for the fact that it was really no longer her childhood bedroom. There was the addition of an elliptical machine and a TV on top of the dresser.

"Keith," the cameraman said, holding out his hand.

Another Keith.

Allison hated the named Keith. The movie producer had also been named Keith. It had been surprising, the first time especially, that he hit her, because she had really liked him in the beginning.

The first time, it was because Allison did not want to go to the restaurant he had chosen. The blow had come out of nowhere, so fast it was as if she had imagined it. He apologized, said that he had a temper, as if somehow that made it okay. The second time, however, was not okay. And then it stopped for more than a year, but happened again when the movie producer, when Keith, did not win an award he'd expected to win. Somehow this gave him the right.

Allison, however, did not hit people when she got angry. She was nice to people, probably much too nice to people. She had been nice, for instance, to that Keith when she broke up with him.

"You are great," she had said, one-hundred-percent lying. Maybe, in her defense, she had been nice because she was worried he would hit her again.

Still, it had been surprisingly easy for Allison to move on. She had managed to pack two suitcases and be gone in less than an hour. She crashed at a friend's house in Silver Lake. The friend had tried to convince her to stay. Then she found the beach house in North Carolina.

"Your name is Keith?" Allison asked the cameraman.

This, after everything else, was a lot to take in. It was not that common a name. How was it that this cameraman was also named Keith?

A thought occurred to Allison. She put down her cheeseburger and checked her backpack.

"Damn," she said, searching her backpack. "Damn. Damn. Damn."

Allison had not packed her charger. It was probably still in the motel room. Allison realized it was ridiculous to be this upset. She could pick up a new one anywhere. At the CVS near the restaurant. Problem solved. She would go there. It was her next plan in life, small as it was.

There was always a new plan. The next thing. That gave her a small measure of comfort.

It sucked, losing her house.

She could allow herself to be upset.

Allison had had only two beers, not enough to be drunk. The idea of it, getting drunk, was appealing to her, but not possible, because she would not drink and drive. Maybe, Allison thought, her life would be better if she did not have a car. She could get as drunk as she wanted to and it would be better for the environment. But her sacrifice would be a drop in the hat. If she didn't have a car, she would be fucked. How could she drive away from the hurricane that was currently her life?

Probably, she would go see her mother next. It felt right. The anniversary of her father's death was coming up; she would finally see her brother's new baby and then she could stop feeling guilty about not having seen her brother's new baby.

And then she would move on from there. She would not remain in New Jersey. Not like her friend Lori, who somehow had ended up back in her parents' house, raising a baby on her own.

There were places Allison could go. It was like that Dr. Seuss book, the one everyone got for graduation.

"What?" the cameraman asked, smiling at her. "Why all the damn-its?"

Allison shrugged.

She had forgotten already.

"It's nothing," she said.

Then she remembered. "I didn't pack my cell phone charger."

It was another ten dollars, more or less—not a big deal. This had been an expensive hurricane overall, that was for sure. Allison felt a wave of sadness come back over her.

She did not want to cry in front of this cameraman. He was a Keith. One of them. It was one thing to cry in front of a TV news camera. At a bar, it was different. It was intimate. It was real.

"I have extra chargers," the cameraman said. "I can give you one. Don't worry."

"That's such a small thing to worry about, isn't it?" Allison said.

She did not move, appalled, when the cameraman wiped a tear that had slid down her cheek. She fought the urge to slap him. He would be upset if she slapped him. It was better not to move.

"You are fine," he said.

It was nice, to hear that spoken out loud.

~~~~~

W here is your car?" she asked the cameraman.

They were standing in the parking lot. It seemed as if Allison was going home with him. But that, she decided, would be okay. It was okay to trust other human beings, the male race included. He had told her, as she ate her cheeseburger, that he had a comfortable guest room, much nicer than the motel.

The cameraman pointed to a sleek racing bike locked to a bicycle rack. There was a helmet attached to the bike and he put it on.

"I love this bike," he said.

"You ride it at night? A bike?"

"I also might have a couple of DWIs."

This made more sense to Allison.

This Keith, fortunately, looked better on a bike than he did on the ground. Then he'd told her about the DWIs and she was not sure again.

Yes, no. Up, down. It would probably be smarter to pay for the not-so-nice motel. Maybe she would find her charger there. But then, Allison would have to check in to the room again, pull out her credit card, write down the license plate of her car. It all seemed like too much.

Allison agreed that she would follow him home.

"I just need to get a new charger," she said, pointing to the CVS. It was, unfortunately, located on the other side of the street.

Still, that had been her next new plan.

"Don't bother," he said. "Like I told you. I have a drawer full of them at home."

Allison frowned.

"Save your money," the cameraman said. "Besides, it's on the other side of the road."

This was true.

Then he got on his bike and quickly disappeared from sight.

Allison had a choice to make. He was surprisingly fast. Allison followed him. She did not follow her plan, but she was already completely off course, so that would have to be okay.

A new cell phone charger was not much of a plan, really.

~~~~~

At the cameraman's house, unsurprisingly, they tried to have sex, even though Allison had told the cameraman it would not happen.

Then, after a whiskey, Allison figured why not. Maybe that would be nice. Sometimes it could be nice.

A distraction.

The cameraman could not get it up.

And that was a relief, really.

Allison had understood her mistake right away, with the first kiss, surprised by the fact that somehow his lips felt old. She had not known that that was possible, but his lips were dried out, wrinkled. The wrong texture for lips.

Still, Allison had done her part, using her hands. She drew the line when he asked if she might try her mouth. There was no way. "No," she said. "I am tired."

It had been such a cute house, her beach house. A dream house. She had not realized until then how sad she was, how tired and sad. She could have had fast bad sex, but not slow bad sex. Allison had her limits.

The house had been Allison's dream and it was gone.

"I could take a pill," the cameraman said. "Wait a second," he said. "I'll be right back."

Allison really wished his name wasn't Keith.

She should have walked out of the restaurant the second she heard his name.

Allison politely declined.

"I am really tired," she said again. "I lost my house today."

"Would you like to sleep in the guest room?" he asked.

That had been the original deal, after all.

"That would be great," Allison said. "Thank you."

"Of course you're tired. I'm sorry. I should have just let you sleep. None of this kissing business. My bad. I hope you don't hate me."

Allison would have hated him if they had kept on trying.

"You said you have a charger?" she asked him.

Allison remembered that she had not returned her mother's calls. She had sent her an email from her phone from the motel the night before, saying that she was fine. Not to worry. This, of course, was not adequate. Her mother would be worried. But her mother would not be happy to know that Allison was drunk in a strange cameraman's house. Maybe it was for the best that her cell phone was dead.

Allison's eyes were closing despite herself. She could call her mother in the morning.

"Oh gosh, it's somewhere," the cameraman said. "I tell you what. It's late. Let me show you the bedroom. You'll like it. I promise I'll find the charger in the morning."

This was not okay, not even close to okay. But her mother had to know that she was fine. Because if she wasn't fine, the police would have called her by now. That was the way her mother thought about things. This thought would give her mother comfort.

The cameraman kissed her on the forehead and that was

fine, even though Allison would have liked to pretend that their brief sexual episode had not happened.

That was the problem with men. They couldn't just be nice.

Allison followed the cameraman to the guest room like a child.

The guest room was surprisingly nice, like Keith said it would be. The comforter was white. The pillows were fluffy. The guest room was one thousand times nicer than his actual bedroom, which was a mess, what one might expect from an older guy who lived alone.

The spare bedroom was, by contrast, like a four-star hotel. It had its own bathroom, and the bathroom was filled with sample-sized toiletries. Lotion, shampoo, conditioner, bath gel, face wash. The room pleased Allison. It was bland and soothing and much nicer than the motel.

For a moment, Allison felt lucky. In a way, she thought, she'd done well for herself. She had, after all, made it through another day.

This one had been especially long.

⌇⌇⌇⌇

*A*llison woke up in a strange bed, a nice bed, and remembered that she did not have a house. Her house had been blue, a pretty shade of light blue. She rubbed her eyes.

A week and a half.

Allison had had the house for a week and a half.

That was a very short amount of time. It had taken her longer to drive cross-country, though she had taken her time, making various stops along the way.

She had slept surprisingly well. There was a digital clock on the bedside table. The time was 11:15 a.m. When did she ever sleep this late? Never. She never did. It was strange to wake up somewhere new for the second day in a row.

It had been a nice house. A sweet house. It was also just a house. Allison reached for her cell phone on the bedside table, but it was dead. That was really stupid. She should have gone to the CVS. Listened to her own voice.

Allison did not even know where she was, exactly: a cameraman's house somewhere in North Carolina. She had driven there, but she did not know the address. She had driven carefully, following the cameraman on his bike, squinting in the dark on the small, unlit roads, worried she might run him over.

Allison remembered the botched attempt to have sex. At least that was over.

It was a new day.

She was fine.

She had her health.

It was like a running joke in her head.

~~~~~

There was no one in Keith's living room.

She walked through it and into the kitchen. There was a fresh pot of coffee in the coffeemaker, a plain white mug on the kitchen counter. Allison poured herself a cup. She opened the refrigerator. She found half-and-half. She poured it into her coffee.

She wondered whether she was alone in the house.

Cameraman was a real job. Maybe he was out at work, shooting more hurricane damage.

She would drink her coffee and she would get on the road.

"Hello?" she called out. "Good morning? Keith?"

It felt strange to say his name out loud. She did not like to say the name out loud, but she also did not want to startle him if he was home.

She did not want to be startled.

He had *seemed* nice, at least. Or not entirely awful. She would not be there if she had not lost her house, but she had had one-night stands before. This was not the stupidest thing she had ever done. Even if it had been a while. Years. The coffee, at least, tasted good.

"In my office," Keith's voice called out, and Allison followed it. She was wearing pink pajama bottoms, an oversized T-shirt she liked to sleep in. This felt too intimate, but the night before she had been briefly almost naked with this man. Sex was such an extraordinary thing, being naked with someone else. The cameraman had been a stranger.

Allison decided at that moment that she would never have a one-night stand again. She felt very good about this decision, though nothing bad had happened to her. Sometimes it was important not to push your luck.

She found the cameraman at a large desk in front of a computer, a huge Apple monitor, looking at a picture of her. It was disturbing to see her own image on the screen. On it she was frozen, standing in front of the place where her house had been. It was eerie, seeing herself like that, the cameraman looking at her, Allison looking at him, looking at her. There was an orange and white cat sitting on the back of his office chair, another one on his lap.

Allison remembered now: coming into the cameraman's house, him greeting his cats, and how she had felt reassured.

"Good morning," Allison said.

It felt incredibly creepy that he was watching her on his computer screen.

"Good morning, Sunshine. You slept in. That's wonderful. You must have needed the sleep. I see you found the coffee. Let me make you breakfast."

Allison looked at herself on the screen. Was that what she looked like? Distressed. Sunburned. Her eyes were wide, teary.

"I am going to have to get on the road soon," Allison said. "Did you find a charger, by any chance?"

"A charger, no," he said. "Not yet."

This did not seem believable. There he was, in a room filled with state-of-the-art computer equipment. Still, she would not contradict him. It was not necessary. She would go back to the CVS and buy a charger. She could get one at a gas station, even. They sold them everywhere.

"I have to go," Allison said.

"What is the hurry?" the cameraman asked.

Allison shrugged.

She did not have to, would not, explain anything to him.

"You've been through a shock," he said. "Let me make you breakfast. Why don't you take a shower? I'll find a charger."

"I can at least check my email on my computer," Allison said. "I have to write to my mother. I know she is worried. Can you give me the wireless password?"

"Ah," Keith said. "The Internet is out. The hurricane. You know how it is."

"Seriously?"

"No reception."

This was starting to feel like the setup to a horror movie. Cell phone dead, Internet out. No one knew where Allison was.

But the cameraman was harmless. He had proven that last night. He rode a bike. He had cats. People with cats were nice.

"It happens all the time," he said. "I have T-Mobile. The worst. I need to get a new provider. I keep telling myself that. You know how that is."

"I need to get in touch with my mother," Allison said. "She must be worried about me."

"Of course she is," Keith said. "It's incredibly frustrating. Not having service. It happens with every storm. I wish I still had a landline. Let me make you breakfast and then we'll drive into town. I make a mean frittata. What kind of cheese do you like? I've got cheddar. Parmesan. Swiss."

Allison shook her head.

"You need to eat something. Are eggs too heavy? How about granola? Fruit? Yogurt?"

"I am good with coffee," Allison said. "I've got to get going."

She watched the cameraman stroke the cat on his lap.

The cat looked at Allison, jumped off the cameraman's lap, and wandered over to her feet. Allison petted the cat. It was a large cat, enormous, really.

"He likes you," Keith said.

Allison nodded.

"He doesn't like everyone," Keith said.

There was the other cat on the back of the chair, wrapped nearly around Keith's neck. It was a little bit creepy. This was all getting much too creepy.

"How many cats do you have?" Allison asked.

"This is it. Just the two."

The conversation ended there.

"So, breakfast?" Keith said.

"I would have some fruit," Allison said. The cameraman seemed to want her to eat breakfast. "And then I have to go."

"Perfect," he said.

The cameraman got up. Walking past her, he kissed Allison quickly on the mouth, a butterfly kiss, before she had a chance to stop him. Last night had been last night. There would be no more kissing. It felt to Allison like the cameraman should have known that, but somehow, he didn't. She followed him into the kitchen. He opened his refrigerator. He had a double package of raspberries. Blueberries. Strawberries. It was a lot of fruit.

"Don't you love Costco?" he said.

Allison did not. Costco made Allison anxious. It was too big. Too loud. Allison found the place overwhelming. But her father had loved Costco. She would go there with him and he would push the large cart, leaning on it instead of on a walker.

Allison had been a surprise baby. Her father had been almost fifty when she was born, her mother in her forties. Her brother was ten years older than she was. Allison's brother liked shopping at Costco. He bought shiny appliances there and winter jackets. Allison, on the other hand, liked to buy expensive produce at farmers markets. Flowers. She sometimes spent a lot of money on flowers.

"Is something wrong?" Keith asked.

"No," Allison said, but, of course, there was.

The cameraman did not have a charger. The cameraman also looked significantly older in the morning light. Not old enough to be her father, but also too old to be someone Allison would kiss.

Allison had made a mistake. That was okay. She would forgive herself.

Allison wondered why she was being so polite.

She wanted to run, get the hell out of the house. But that was overreacting. She would be on the road soon.

Keith put the fruit into a plain white ceramic bowl.

He had good taste in bowls, like he did in bedspreads. He was not awful. Allison said this to herself, like a mantra, as if saying it made it true.

"Would you like some yogurt?" he asked her. "I have Greek yogurt."

Allison shook her head.

"I am trying to be nice to you," he said.

"I appreciate that," Allison said. "Thank you for the coffee. I just feel like I have to get going."

"I just took a pill," the cameraman said. "So we can try again if you'd like."

"Um. I would rather not," Allison said, looking down into her coffee. She was shocked by this announcement, but she pretended not to be. The sentence hung in the air, as if the cameraman required an explanation.

"Last night, I had been drinking," Allison said.

"You were not that drunk," the cameraman said.

"Nevertheless," Allison said.

She had known that his name was a bad sign and had gone home with him anyway. From the living room window, she could see a creek at the end of his small lawn, and on the other side of the creek there were woods. There had been a road nearby, she recalled. She was not in the middle of nowhere. The drive to his house had felt like forever, but Allison realized that had been because of the bicycle.

There were twists, there were turns. There had been no streetlights. At one point, he had gone so fast that she'd lost him. She had seen a family of deer staring at her from the side of the road. Maybe the deer had been a sign, too.

Allison's cell phone was dead. No one knew where she was. That was unfortunate. In her own horror film, the one she had written, the protagonist's cell phone was dead. Allison hated the way cell phones now played such a big part in film and television plots.

"I appreciate your letting me sleep here last night. But—" Here the cameraman cut her off.

"You are most welcome," he said. "It's my pleasure to have you."

"But," Allison went on, "like I told you. I need to get going."

"You have somewhere to go?"

"Yes."

The presumption that she didn't irritated Allison. Even though she had absolutely nowhere she needed to be. That was beside the point. "Of course I do. I have a life, after all."

"But your house blew down."

It really did feel like the Three Little Pigs. And that would make the cameraman the Big Bad Wolf. Even if he had not caused the hurricane. He was a small man. He was not a threat. He had a bicycle. Cats. But Allison's worry at this point had become real. Would she really have to explain that no meant no?

This was awkward, more than a little bit uncomfortable, but that was all that it was. The cameraman was not a straight-out rapist; he was just an asshole. There was a significant difference.

"Exactly," Allison said. "My house blew down and now I have to pick up the pieces."

"The pieces of your house are blown all over North Carolina."

"I am aware of that," Allison said. "I am not being literal." She wondered, *Was that right?* So many people used the word *literal* the wrong way. "My house blew down and so I have a lot to do. I have to file an insurance claim. I have to get a cell phone charger. I have to make calls. Get on the Internet. I have to call my mother."

"The Internet will come back soon," the cameraman said.

"I am sure it will."

Allison was scared now, but she did not have to be scared.

That was just how she felt. In a few days, she would be back in New Jersey and she would tell her friend Lori the story of how she had almost had a one-night stand with a cameraman named Keith and they would laugh about it.

"You have to stop taking these stupid risks, Allie," her friend would say. Allison would agree.

Allison had traveled to East Africa with a friend after college. In Lamu, a gorgeous island off the coast of Kenya, she had swum on a beach all alone, leaving her passport in her backpack on her beach towel. You could not be more stupid than that, really, but the backpack had not been stolen.

Lori was right. Still, you could get away with things in life. Allison had had sex with an Australian man who owned a hotel on the island, and it had been good. After, he bought her dinner at the hotel restaurant. That part had been wonderful. The meal.

Allison absently ate a raspberry and instantly regretted it. It occurred to Allison that even her coffee could have been poisoned. But she tried to relax. Sure, the cameraman had turned out to be creepy, but he did not take women home after a hurricane and poison them. This could not be a modus operandi. Hurricanes were not *that* common that this could become standard practice. The world had become such a horrible place that it was easy to imagine the worst of another person.

"It was nice to meet you," Allison said. "I've never been on TV before. I'll give you my email and maybe you can send me the footage. And now I have to go."

"Fine," the cameraman said amiably. "That sounds like a plan." He walked into the kitchen, taking her empty coffee cup with him, putting it in the sink. He came back with a heavy glass vase. "I'll email you."

Allison looked at the vase curiously. He did not seem to have any flowers, and she did not know why he had brought it out now. *He has cats,* Allison told herself, because her heart had started to beat quickly.

"Anyway," Allison said. "I am going to get dressed and hit the road. Thank you for the hospitality."

"I don't want you to go."

Allison blinked.

It should not matter what he wanted, the cameraman. Keith. Keith stood next to her, much too close, holding the big glass vase in one hand. He used the other free hand to tilt Allison's face toward him, to kiss her.

Allison turned her head, avoiding his lips.

"No," she said. "Honestly. I cannot be more clear. We are not going to have sex. I have to go."

The cameraman brought the glass vase overhead.

Allison could hear the glass crack. And then she felt it shatter. Shards of glass rained down past her face. They landed in her hair, created a circle of glass around her bare feet.

It was almost beautiful.

"Why did you do that?" she asked.

Then the world turned to black.

*A*llison woke up in the guest room, in the same clean, nice bed she had slept in the night before. Now the white comforter was stained with a long red streak, all the way from the edge of the bed to the pillow. Allison touched the pillowcase. It was soaking wet. It was soaked red. The red was all blood, Allison assumed, her blood, blood formerly safely contained inside her head. It was a dark maroon color. Not a bright red, like when she cut her finger, but darker, more like the blood from her period.

Allison wondered how much blood she had lost. A lot, it seemed like. All of it had come out of her head. She had a head injury. She would need stitches. She could have had a concussion. She could be dying. She did not know. She had never had a head injury before.

She lifted her hands to see if she was somehow tied to the bed. She was not. She did not feel like she was dying, but how could she know?

"Mom," she said, trying out her voice. "Mommy."

But her mother lived far away, in New Jersey. Her mother could not help her. She had not even called her mother after the hurricane to say that she was okay. She was a terrible daughter.

"Ow," Allison said.

She touched her head. Her hair was sticky with blood. There was a spot, an area, really, that was tender. An open wound where her scalp should be.

Tears streamed down Allison's face.

Losing her house made some kind of awful sense. It's what happens when you buy a beach house despite full awareness of rising sea levels. Global warming.

This was worse.

This felt entirely unfair.

Allison was in an actual live-or-die situation, she realized. Only it was gorier, scarier, than the horror movie she wrote. And at the moment, she was moving much too slowly. Allison needed to flee this house as fast as she possibly could, but she also had a head injury, an open wound. Her vision was blurry. She was scared about what she would find on the other side of the door. An orange and white cat was lying on the edge of the bed. Allison reached out her hand and the cat came over to her and she petted it.

"Hey, kitty," Allison said. "Hey, you."

She noticed that the door to her room was slightly ajar. That was a good thing. She was not locked inside this room, at least.

The cat purred. Allison felt in love with this cat. She was tempted to take the cat with her, as protection, maybe, or a reward, a reward for the suffering she had gone through, but that did not make sense, and the cat got up and jumped off the bed anyway. So Allison was alone again.

Allison did not actually want this cat.

She wanted her mother.

Allison sat up slowly, swinging her legs off the bed. Her white T-shirt was covered in blood. So were her pajama bottoms. Should she change into clean clothes before leaving the room or just flee, willy-nilly, barefoot and bloody, to her car? That was what a girl in a movie would do, but that did not necessarily mean it was the best decision.

Allison noticed her backpack on the floor by the bed. She hoped her car keys were still in the front pocket.

"Come on," Allison said to herself, willing herself to move. "Come on, come on."

Her survival, after all, was at stake. Allison was doing a horrible job at saving her life. Shameful, in fact.

For all she knew, the cameraman was on the other side of the door, waiting for her. He probably would not crack another heavy glass vase on top of her head. He had already done that, after all.

It was okay, Allison decided, to use the bathroom before she left the guest room. The room smelled like pee and she realized she had probably peed the bed. Which was humiliating. She very much wanted to rinse her face, look at herself in the mirror. Allison did not know whether she could escape this house if she did not first go to the bathroom. That area of her body felt okay, though. That was reassuring.

She was already failing how to behave in a horror film. She should be searching for a weapon. But what was she going to do, brandish the bedside table lamp like a sword and storm out of the room? She felt too weak to do that, really. She felt weak. She was unsteady. What she needed was a hospital.

She wanted to be rescued.

Sometimes people were rescued.

In movies. On TV.

In real life, no one knew that she was missing, and there was no one to rescue her, anyway. Friends had texted before the hurricane telling her to stay safe. Really, though, she was alone in the world. This made Allison sad. Suddenly, she understood the impulse to get married.

Allison had questioned the motives of friends who had begun to do it, get married, one after another, forcing her to travel to ridiculous places and wear uncomfortable dresses and shoes. She had been to so many weddings in the last couple of years.

She had had an uncomfortable conversation with her brother after his wedding, learning that she had not fulfilled her bridesmaid's duties properly. Allison had never wanted to be a bridesmaid. As sister of the groom, she had not been given much of a choice.

Allison went into the bathroom and peed in the toilet.

She wiped herself carefully. She pulled up her pajama bottoms. She stood and looked at herself in the mirror. What she saw was a little alarming. Her face was a pale shade of greenish gray. There were dark circles under both of her eyes. Her hair was matted, thick with blood, and there were small bits of glass in it. Her eyes were bloodshot, red spiderwebs crisscrossing the whites.

Allison reached for a folded white washcloth, ran it under hot water, pressed it onto her head. It came away red.

Allison left the glass shards in her hair, afraid that she would cut herself trying to get them out. Again, this was probably absolutely the wrong thing to do.

She was spending all this time in the bathroom. Still, somehow it felt right. Washing her face after a violent attack felt like the right thing to do.

She stared at herself in the mirror, and then, without warning, she threw up in the sink. She hadn't had enough time to shift to the toilet. Allison turned on the tap water, rinsing out the sink. Then she proceeded to brush her teeth. Allison's toothbrush was still on the sink from the night before, when she had voluntarily decided to sleep at the cameraman's house.

The police would love that.

But this wasn't rape. It was a vase smashed over her head. Clearly not a matter of he said/she said.

Allison loved her toothpaste, her Tom's of Maine, peppermint and baking soda. Her mouth had tasted sickly, like blood, even before the vomit, but the toothpaste made it better—the mint, her breath cool and clean.

"Hi, Allison," Allison said to her reflection.

It was good to not be dead.

In addition to friends getting married, Allison had friends who were suicidal. She never knew what to say to them. She would try to tell jokes. Now, instead, she would be able to tell them about this moment. How she felt glad to be alive. There was still a small chunk of vomit in the sink. There was blood, her blood, all over her T-shirt. She squinted. It looked like maybe a little bit of her scalp was missing. Was that possible? A little nick in her skull.

But not enough, luckily, for her brains to fall out.

Allison was going slow, much too slow.

She would make a compromise, she told herself.

Even if she could not move quickly, she would move.

"Move," Allison said.

She had gone to the toilet. She had rinsed her face, she'd brushed her teeth. Now, now it was time to go, escape: get into her car and drive to her mother's house, where her childhood bedroom awaited her.

Now she would act with some urgency. She would not change her clothes, say goodbye to the cats. She would grab her dead phone, her backpack that held her car keys, and she would hold these keys like a weapon.

She could stab the cameraman in the eye if she needed to. Even if she did not feel quite secure on her feet. She would stab him. Stab him in the eye. She could do that. That idea made her feel better.

And that was what Allison told herself, leaving the bathroom. *Stab him in the eye.* She was shaking. She walked over to the bed and reached for her phone on the bedside table. She felt a fresh wave of nausea seeing her blood on the pillow, the white pillowcase soaked red, and she vomited again, on top of the pillow, but she did not go back to the bathroom to brush her teeth. She had left her toothpaste and toothbrush in the bathroom, but she would not go back for them. She was moving forward. Not backward. She could replace these items at the CVS.

The CVS. She should have gone to the CVS to get a charger. And then none of this would have happened.

Stab him in the eye, Allison told herself and reached for her backpack. It felt heavy, much heavier than when she had brought it in. But she found her keys, in the front pocket where she always tried to put her keys. That felt like a small miracle. Allison put her phone in her backpack, the backpack on her back, and then she used both hands to hold the keys, hold the keys out in front of her. She was still going slowly. But that was fine. She was being methodical. *Stab him in the eye. Stab him in the eye.*

Stab him in the eye.

Allison pushed open the bedroom door and stepped out

into the living room. Bright light streamed into the room. The cats lay spooned together, on an armchair. Otherwise, the room was empty.

Allison had the impulse to call out to make sure that she had the all clear. But then, recalling the cameraman's name, she felt ashamed. She should have known the second that he told her. Anyway, she did not need to make sure she was safe, because she wasn't. She was going to have to take a risk, or she could end up like the woman in that novel, locked in a basement room for years and years, raising a strange son with a ponytail.

Allison noticed a hole in the wall above the couch that had not been there before, as if the cameraman had taken his fist and punched this hole. There was no other explanation for such a hole. He had not seemed crazy when Allison met him. He had seemed like a balding, skinny man, an eccentric, maybe, but a man with a job, a skill. He had a friendly smile.

He had bought her a cheeseburger. He rode a bike.

He had a cat. Two.

Allison took a step toward the front door.

And then another.

She knew she ought to run, but did not feel like she could run. The backpack was too heavy, but the effort of taking it off was hard to imagine.

Also, she did not want to drop it, damage her computer.

On the table where the cameraman attacked her the day before was a glass vase filled with flowers.

It must have been a different vase. There was a note propped up against it, a piece of paper folded in half, with her name on it. In front of that, there lay a cell phone charger.

With her keys out in front of her, Allison walked to the table. She picked up the note and she read it. Allison was failing, again, to rush from the house. But the note was addressed to her. She was too curious not to read it.

Allison, the note said. *I am so sorry. I went off my meds. My ex-wife told me I could never, ever go off my meds again, and now I know that she is right. I am checking myself into a hospital. There is food in the refrigerator. Please help yourself. You will need your strength. I left food for the cats and someone will be coming to feed them tomorrow, but if you want to refill their water bowl and give them a fresh can of wet food that would be terrific. Thank you.*

Allison read and reread the note.

The cameraman was gone. There was food for her in the refrigerator. There were cats on the armchair, happily asleep.

Did he really expect her to feed them?

"Stab him in the eye," Allison said out loud, but that seemed a little bit silly now.

She walked into the kitchen, looked out the kitchen window. She was not in the wilderness. There was the driveway, a paved road that would lead her back to the highway. The cameraman's van was not there.

Allison saw her car. It was a good car. Many years ago, after college, her mother had given her this silver car and bought herself a new one, a slightly better model.

The sky was a clear, bright blue.

Allison picked up the cats' water bowl, even though it was not empty, and refilled it. She would not give them wet food. There was plenty of food for them already, extra bowls filled with extra food. And wet food was too much like vomit.

It was scary, taking the first step, and then the step after that, one after the next, out the cameraman's door. Allison had an idea that he could still come at her from the bushes. That would make an audience scream.

She might not get out that easy.

It was still hurricane season.

She touched the tender spot on her head. She knew that she should not touch it.

Allison walked all the way to her car.

She could hear the birds chirping, feel the sun on her face. She was alone.

The cameraman was not lurking. He was gone. He was in a mental hospital.

Allison clicked on the button on her key chain and heard the door unlock. The world had not changed in two nights. For instance, her car keys still worked. She got into her unlocked car, laid her heavy backpack on the passenger seat. She took a deep breath, wiped the sweat off her forehead with her hand.

She put her key in the ignition. The car started to beep, the noise so loud that, for a moment, Allison felt herself black out. The pain in her head was excruciating. The beeping would not stop; it would not stop. Then she remembered and put on her seat belt.

The beeping stopped.

Thank God, thank God, thank God, she thought.

Still, Allison did not drive.

She did not know where she was.

She had not taken the cameraman's charger, the one he'd left on the table. She wanted nothing from him.

But there was a cell phone charger in her car.

Of course. It had been there all along.

Allison plugged in her cell phone. The phone was still dead, but she was not dead.

The blue light on her phone turned on. The phone was charging.

"Stab him in the eye," she said, just to hear the sound of her own voice.

She was glad that she had not been required to do that.

She touched the top of her head again, felt the exposed spot on her skull. It was soft. It was a little gooey.

She was not dead.

She had her health.

"Hi, Allison," she said, and she took a deep breath.

Allison put her foot on the gas, and she started to drive.

~~~~~

Part
Two

At a rest stop on the turnpike, Allison stopped to get a Starbucks coffee and thought to herself, maybe everything was going to be fine. She had money, a wallet, a working cell phone. She was part of the human race.

Only people were staring at her. Keeping a distance. Allison had not changed out of her bloodstained clothes. Her long hair was matted with blood, sticking to her head. Probably the glass was still there, making her hazardous not only to herself but to others. She had thought it was a good decision, getting out of the cameraman's house alive. It was not, however, a good decision in terms of a public appearance.

"Jesus. What happened to you?" the woman who took her Starbucks order asked her. She had pink hair. Her name tag said Missy. Allison was surprised that anyone would actually go by this name, but there it was. "Look at your head. I can see your brain!"

Allison shrugged.

"I am fine," she said.

She was fine.

She had driven all the way to this Starbucks, after all.

She still had her health.

But Missy did not look convinced. Allison wondered if her brain was actually showing. That could not be good. She thought the hole was mainly covered by the blood clot that clumped her hair. She thought that only the idea of a hole in her head was visible. Not the hole itself.

"I got smashed over the head with a glass vase," Allison explained.

This was probably the worst thing that had ever happened to her. She had been on a roll up until then. She had sold a script. She had an agent who wanted to get her more writing gigs. Her script was out in the world now, a film currently in production. Allison wondered how it was doing. Whether she would go to the premiere. Who she would take with her. Not the movie producer. She had left him. Sometimes Allison was still surprised that she had done that.

She would never have such a nice swimming pool again.

For a moment, Allison forgot where she was. She wanted to go home, swim in the movie producer's pool. Wherever she was, the air-conditioning was turned on high, and Allison wished she had thought to wear a sweater. Carefully, Allison touched the hole in her head, the goopy spot, which was still goopy but had begun to crust around the edges with dried blood. Apparently, it was noticeable. Missy, the Starbucks girl, was staring at her, making Allison want to say something rude about *her* hair. Pink hair was strangely popular these days. Allison did not understand why.

"A man," Allison said, remembering her boyfriend in Los Angeles, trying to remember why she had left him. She could see his swimming pool, the water sparkling, the landscaped flowers surrounding the pool. "Keith."

She blinked. She made a fist and then unclenched her hand. Perhaps she was not fine. She remembered the cameraman coming out of the kitchen, holding that vase. His name was also Keith. The drive so far had actually not been fine. Her head did not feel quite right. She blinked constantly.

It occurred to her, at this Starbucks on the turnpike, that at some point she had forgotten she had been attacked. She had gone into a sort of twilight state. She had concentrated on driving at the speed limit, not over, not under, not swerving from her lane, never changing lanes, except to exit for the rest stop. That had felt, somehow, like an enormous risk in itself.

But Allison was moving, one step at a time, going home, that was where she was going.

Getting coffee at Starbucks was just a part of that process.

"He was angry at me," Allison said slowly. She realized she should not still be talking to Missy. She was holding up the line. "I wouldn't sleep with him."

"Holy shit," Missy said. "Have you called the police?"

Allison shook her head.

That had not occurred to her.

She had been attacked.

She should call the police.

"Not yet," she said. "I should, shouldn't I?"

"Damn straight," Missy said. "Call them now."

"I will do that," Allison said.

But she wanted to go home first.

"You need to go to the hospital."

"I will do that, too."

"Girl, your head is wide open."

Allison did not like being called Girl, but she would not tell Missy her actual name, either.

She struggled to open the app on her phone to pay for the coffee, but she couldn't find it, and then she did find it, but she was not logged in. The app wanted her password.

"I don't know my password," Allison whispered.

Allison understood that she was going to cry.

She did not want to make all of this conversation. She wanted her coffee.

Missy had the coffee in her hand.

"Don't worry about it," Missy said.

"Really?" Allison was so grateful for the small kindness. She took her coffee, her croissant. She found the half-and-half. She took her first sip of her coffee.

It was good, her Starbucks coffee. Sometimes Starbucks coffee wasn't; it could be too strong, overbrewed, but this one was fine. Allison was happy about that.

This was not quite the same thing, Allison realized, as looking at the silver lining. Still, it was a good thing. Allison sat at a table and ate her croissant. It was warm and texture-less and delicious.

Allison googled Driving with Head Injuries on her phone. She was not surprised to discover that it was not advised, but she had already driven one hundred miles. She was not going to stop now. Allison closed her eyes and could see the orange and white cats.

A little boy holding his mother's hand pointed at Allison.

"Look, Mommy," he said. "That lady. She's all bloody."

Allison worried that they would come over, try to help her, but they kept on walking. Allison wondered if someone else would stop and help her if she remained at this rest stop for much longer. Allison very much did not want that. She wanted to go home.

A hospital, the police, that would all slow her down, and so she walked back to her car, taking her coffee with her. She was grateful for the coffee.

Allison had trouble finding her car in the parking lot. It was a silver car in what seemed like a sea of silver cars, but she had a moment of inspiration and clicked on a button on her key, and the lights on her car flashed and beeped and she was able to find it.

"Good girl," she told herself, and got into her car.

She blacked out, again, when the car started to beep before she put on her seat belt, but this time at least Allison knew what it was.

"Motherfucking car," she said.

She put on her seat belt.

Sometimes, on the long drive, Allison thought that the whole world was on fire. Other times, she thought it was beeping. Which seemed just as bad.

Allison had not actually opened the article about driving with head injuries. She knew, of course, that it would tell her not to drive. She already knew the risks. She could pass out behind the wheel and kill herself. Worse, she could kill a busload full of children like in a movie she had seen a long time ago. More likely, Allison would drink her Starbucks coffee, stay in the right lane, and be in New Jersey before dark.

~~~~~

Allison's mother hugged her hard.

Then her mother proceeded to yell at her. It was not the homecoming Allison had been hoping for.

"What happened to you?"

Her mother's voice was loud. Allison could hear her mother's dog barking.

"I've been calling and calling. I've been so worried. I called the police. They told me you weren't a missing person. There was nothing they could do." Tears were running down Allison's mother's cheeks. "Why didn't you call me? I have been so worried."

"You are yelling at me, Mom," Allison said. "Please stop. Please. Please."

It made her head, which already hurt so much, hurt even more. Allison put her hands on her ears. She disentangled herself from her mother's embrace and sat down on the first step of the staircase, which was what she always had to do when she came home.

The dog insisted on it.

Allison petted her mother's barking dog.

"Hi, Gibson," she said. "Hi, little dog."

Before anything else, she had to calm the dog down.

"I am fine, Mom," Allison said, still petting the dog. "I

want to take a shower and go to sleep. I've been driving all day. I can explain everything tomorrow."

"What about the house?" her mother said. "Your house."

Allison blinked, not sure what her mother was talking about. She was home.

"The house?" her mother said. "Your beach house? The hurricane?"

Allison remembered. Her house. Her dream house. She hadn't told her mother about the house yet. She hadn't spoken to her mother since before the hurricane. She should have responded to her mother's messages. It had not been intentional. Her cell phone had died. The cameraman had promised to find her a charger.

"Is there anything to eat?" Allison asked.

Sometimes when she came home her mother got her turkey sandwiches from the kosher deli, but she hadn't told her mother that she was coming home. Her mother was not a mind reader. Allison was not hungry, anyway. She did not know why she asked.

"Are you hungry? Why didn't you tell me you were coming home? There's no food in the house."

Allison kept on petting her mother's dog. Gibson was calming down. He was licking Allison's fingers. He was a good dog, even if he was loud. There was never any food in the house.

"I have apples," her mother told her.

"Shh," Allison said, petting the small white dog. For no reason, he had taken a step back and started barking at Allison again. "I am petting you, shh, please be quiet. Please, Gibson."

Now Allison was crying, tears streaming down her cheeks. She did not understand it. It was the noise, Gibson barking. It was all too much.

Allison's mother watched, aghast.

"What happened to you, sweetheart?" her mother said.

She looked at Allison closely for the first time. "Why are you covered in blood? What happened to your head? There is a hole in your head, Allison! WHAT HAPPENED TO YOU?"

Allison did not respond. She did not know what to say. Her mother, like the pink-haired Starbucks girl Missy, was going to try to make her go to the hospital.

She should not have gone home. She was not sure where her friend Lori lived anymore. Of course, she went home. The dog had not stopped barking.

"Can you make him stop?" Allison said.

Allison's mother took Allison's hand. She pulled her up from the steps and embraced her again.

"Mom," Allison said.

That was all she wanted.

She had driven nearly eight straight hours for that.

"Baby," her mother said. "I don't understand. I don't think you understand, but something terrible happened to you."

The dog was *still* barking, jumping on the backs of Allison's legs, scratching her. "Damn it, Gibson," Allison said before she could stop herself, which she knew was a bad thing, because her mother loved the dog fiercely.

Somehow, Allison's mother let this comment go. She had wrapped Allison in her arms and did not let go. It turned out this was not what Allison wanted, after all. She wanted to pee. She wanted her turkey sandwich.

"It's going to be okay," her mother said, which was what Allison thought, too. She had made it home.

Her mother did not sound convinced.

~~~~~

Somehow, without even realizing it, Allison found herself in the front seat of her mother's car. Her mother was leaning over her, buckling her seat belt.

"Where are we going?" Allison asked. "I want to take a shower," she said. "I need to pee. Let's not go anywhere, please, Mom? I just got home. I drove for such a long time."

Her life, Allison realized, was still a horror movie. Even now, in New Jersey. Somehow, Allison couldn't get out of it. Her mother pulled out of the driveway, but she had not put on her seat belt. The car was beeping. Beeping. Beeping. It would not stop beeping.

"Mom." Allison put her hands over her ears. She felt her hair, crusted in blood. This was almost as bad as being in the cameraman's house. She had thought everything would be all better once she got out.

She had bought a house, Allison remembered, a perfect little blue house by the beach. She had loved that house. It was her house. All hers.

"Put your seat belt on," she begged her mother. "Please."

"I always forget," her mother said, as if the pain she had inflicted upon her daughter was of no concern. Allison's mother was going deaf. She did not hear the beeping. "It's a short drive," her mother said.

Slowly, much too slowly, Allison's mother put on her seat belt.

The beeping stopped.

"Good," Allison said.

Her mother looked confused.

Allison leaned her head back and closed her eyes. She knew where she was being taken. The hospital where her father had died. Whenever she came home, Allison made a point of not driving on the street that took her past this hospital. It was a place she did not ever want to go back to, and her mother was taking her there. "Mom," she said once more, but she did not have the energy to protest.

She knew what she looked like. She had registered the alarm on Missy's face. Missy had meant to be kind. Allison touched the spot on the top of her head and it was still gooey. She had a hole in her head.

Once, in a creative writing class back in college, another student had written a short story called "Like a Hole in Your Head," and Allison thought it was one of the worst short stories ever written.

"Don't touch it!" her mother screamed.

She was being loud, again, her mother. Her mother did not understand. Allison looked at her mother's face and saw that she was afraid. Terrified, even.

"I did not mean to yell," her mother said. "We're going to be at the hospital soon and they will take care of you, honey. Don't touch your head. Your hands could be dirty. I don't think you should touch it. Tell me what happened, Allison. How did this happen to you?"

Allison did not answer.

Somehow Allison had fallen asleep while her mother was talking to her, and her mother had started shaking her, slapping her shoulder as she drove. A car honked at them, loud, the driver laying her hand on the horn and not letting go. It was so loud. Allison opened her eyes to see where the noise was coming from, but at least that made her mother stop shaking her.

"Wake up! Wake up!" her mother screamed. The noise level inside the car was out of control. "You could have a concussion, sweetheart. A concussion. Do you understand you could die? We are almost there. I can't believe you drove all the way from North Carolina. What were you thinking? Why didn't you call me?"

Allison wanted to ask her mother to be quiet, but she was afraid that would make her mother angry at her, make her yell even louder. She was afraid that her mother would kill her before they even made it to the hospital, and Allison did not want to die. That was not really a possibility, anyway, even though her mother was freaking out. She was going to close her eyes again, just for a second, but her mother punched her shoulder and it hurt.

"This is crazy," Allison said. "Be nice to me."

"We are here," her mother said. "Don't even think about falling asleep again."

Her mother signaled left and she was pulling into the hospital parking lot. Allison remembered hating this parking lot. She hated it. She hated paying the exorbitant parking fee, having to look for spots in the multitiered, narrow garage. When she visited her father, she drove around the neighborhood instead, finding free parking spaces on side streets four or five blocks away. She would walk slowly to the hospital. She hated this hospital. She hated the white grand piano in the lobby and the man who sometimes played it.

Fortunately, her mother did not park the car. She went straight to the emergency room entrance, put on her blinkers, and took Allison straight in.

That, at least, was something.

Allison wanted to sit down on the plastic seats and wait, but her mother took her straight up to the counter and started screaming at the woman at the desk, who was on the phone. "Help my daughter, she is hurt, she is bleeding. Help her!"

"Mom," Allison said. She kept her arms at her sides. She did not want to touch the hole in her head and get yelled at again. "Please. You are so loud."

Someone came, and Allison was put in a wheelchair and wheeled away.

Allison did not like it.

"I swear I am fine," she protested. "I can walk. Give me a fucking break with this wheelchair. I can walk."

She was not listened to. She was wheeled away, taken deeper into the hospital that had killed her father.

It sucked, coming all this way, and then not being listened to. Her mother could have let her take a shower, at least. Allison knew she looked bad. And maybe that was all that it was, not an emergency. Allison wondered what she could have done differently. And then she felt herself pee in her pants, stuck in a wheelchair she did not need. It was the second time in two days.

The humiliations were piling up on top of themselves, one after another.

All the fight was out of her.

"I'm sorry, Mommy," Allison said. "I'm sorry. I'm so sorry."

"You have nothing to be sorry about," her mother said, next to her, holding her hand. "You're in the hospital. They are going to take care of you. I promise."

It was, of course, the hospital where her father died. And they were supposed to take care of him, too.

〰〰〰

*T*here was an Asian doctor talking to her.

He was cute. An incredibly pretty face for a man. Brown eyes. A small, perfect nose. Thin lips. Medium height. Incredibly familiar. Maybe that was what she liked right away. She felt like she could trust him.

Allison smiled at him. She had known someone in college who had looked a lot like this doctor. Danny Yang. She had fooled around with him a couple of times, but he was in a long-distance relationship with someone else, and, besides that, he was not her type. Not because he was Asian, or because he was an inch shorter than her. No, it was because he was so straitlaced that it never went beyond that, though he offered to break up with his girlfriend if she asked him to.

Danny Yang, from college, had wanted to be a doctor, but he had struggled with organic chemistry, so he double-majored in economics to keep his options open. No matter what, he told her, he'd make money; there was no point in an expensive liberal arts education without some kind of guarantee. He had made fun of Allison for majoring in English. Her life, he had warned her, would go nowhere with that useless degree. It turned out that Danny's girlfriend had been cheating on him. He did not have all the answers, though he liked to think so.

That was what it was like in college.

No one in a long-distance relationship worked out. The ones who stayed in these relationships, who got married right out of college and had babies, were invariably boring. Or they got divorced. Whereas Allison, before her movie producer, had never bothered with relationships.

Allison stared at her cute doctor, fascinated. He really did look like an older, more attractive Danny. It was wild. She could not examine him properly because he was peering into her eyes with a flashlight. This was incredibly annoying.

"Follow my finger with your eyes," he instructed her.

Allison did what she was told. Danny Yang, in college, he had fingers, too. She read the name tag on his white doctor's coat: Dr. Daniel Yang.

It made sense, after all, why the doctor looked like Danny Yang. The doctor was Danny Yang. But now, Allison did not feel comfortable that this Danny Yang was also her doctor. She did not want him to see her in New Jersey, and not like this.

They used to talk into the middle of the night. They would talk about their future lives. Hopes and dreams. Kids they would have. Trips they would take. All of that bullshit. They were never, ever going to live in New Jersey. He was from the next town over.

"Can you tell me your name?" he asked her now. "Can you count backward from one hundred?"

It was him, of course. She knew his voice. She knew his eyes. She wished that she had been nicer to him in the end. She had been bitter when he came to her *after* he had been dumped, wanting only then for them to really be together. She had let him know how lame that was.

She hadn't thought about Danny in a long time.

She wondered what they were doing there, now, in this hospital. Her father had died almost a year ago. She did not understand, really, why she was there. There was no reason to be there anymore.

She racked her brain but, unfortunately, her brain felt fuzzy. For instance, she did not remember going to the hospital, yet she appeared to be wearing a hospital gown.

"It's me, Danny," Allison said.

He was looking into her eyes with a flashlight, but he had not truly seen her yet.

"It's Allison. College Allison. I guess I have looked better or you might recognize me. Do you really want me to count for you?"

Allison figured she might as well count for him, but then she forgot what he had asked her to do. And then she remembered. He wanted her to count backward, but she did not feel like it. It did not seem like this should be their first conversation after so many years. Counting backward was a dumb thing to ask her to do, anyway. Also, it seemed hard.

Allison wondered why they hadn't decided to meet for coffee or a drink. A better place to catch up. Wasn't that what people did?

Daniel Yang, the doctor, lowered his flashlight.

"Allison?" he said. "It that you? Jesus! What happened to you? Are you okay?"

Allison laughed.

It was funny, after all, for him to ask whether she was okay. He was the doctor. He was a *doctor*. It was good that he was a doctor. That was all he'd ever wanted to be. His mother would be happy. His mother was not interested in finance. Doctor or lawyer—that was all she wanted for him.

Danny, of course, shouldn't have been *Allison's* doctor.

He was looking at her with too much affection.

"It's been such a long time," Allison said to him.

It seemed stupid, now, that they had ever stopped speaking.

Another doctor was now leaning over her head, examining the wound. Danny was her doctor. Allison's head was none of her business.

"Can you tell us what happened, Allison?" the other doctor asked.

This doctor had a Russian accent. Allison remembered her father complaining about all the different ethnicities in his medical team. He'd had an Indian doctor and he could not understand her accent. It had seemed racist, her father's gripe, but it was true that his doctor could have slowed down, she could have made sure that he understood.

Her father had been so confused about what was happening to him. He did not understand when the doctors tried to explain his condition to him. This had not made full sense to Allison then. Now she understood better how he'd felt. She remembered arriving home, petting her mother's dog, asking for a turkey sandwich. Nothing about a hospital. The doctor with the Russian accent was asking her a question, but Allison had been unable to focus.

Allison looked at Danny. She did not want to talk to the woman doctor with the Russian accent. She wanted Danny.

Danny was holding her hand.

"You're a doctor?" she asked him.

"A neurosurgeon."

"That's amazing," Allison said. "I didn't know you were interested in the brain."

"It just sort of happened," Danny said.

Allison nodded.

The brain. Her hand was clearly not vital to neurosurgery. Holding it was unprofessional. But Allison was glad.

There was also a nurse in the room, checking an IV that had been put in her arm. It felt like time was moving both fast and slow. Allison realized she was hooked up to all sorts of machines, but she remembered none of it, IVs, being transferred to a hospital bed.

"Tell us what happened, honey," the nurse said.

Allison loved to be called honey. The nurse, a Black woman with a Jamaican accent, was nice. Allison could tell who was nice right away. Well, usually.

And her accent was beautiful. Even Allison's father would have liked it, liked her. Nurses tended to be so much nicer than the doctors. It was the doctors who killed you, the doctors who had killed her father.

Allison closed her eyes, trying to remember. There had to be a reason why she was here. How she had gotten here, without her consent.

"I was hit on the head with a glass vase," Allison said, remembering. "Could that be why I'm here?"

Though she could not see her, Allison heard her mother gasp. So her mother was in the room. It was her mother who had brought her here. Allison shouldn't have come home. That was what had happened. She had come home after her house had been flattened by a hurricane.

Allison had not meant to upset her mother, who was still grieving her father. It was not fair to be back here, to have done this to her mother. She could have stayed in North Carolina, rebuilt her house. Her movie producer boyfriend used to tell her that she did not see things all the way through. That was why she had finished that screenplay and sold it, just to prove him wrong.

"That explains the glass in her hair," the Jamaican nurse said.

"I have glass in my hair?" Allison asked.

"Has anyone taken any pictures?" the nurse asked, seeming unsurprised that the answer was no. The nurse pulled out her cell phone and started snapping photos of Allison's head. Allison wondered why the nurse would want pictures of her head. She wished the nurse had asked her permission. She was not in the mood to have her picture taken.

Danny's expression told her how bad she looked. She wanted to tell Danny that she was still pretty, that he'd just caught her on a bad day.

"It's going to be okay, honey," the nurse told Allison.

Allison appreciated the nurse's confidence.

Of course she'd be okay.

She thought of telling Danny Yang to let go of her hand, not because she actually wanted him to, but because that was what he *should* do, and she did not want him to get into trouble at his job. And especially not on her account. He looked *so* worried.

Allison had always known he was in love with her.

"You got hit on the head with a vase?" Allison's mother said, her voice still much too loud. "I don't understand. Did this happen in the hurricane? Do you mean you were hit over the head with a tree branch?"

"It's fine, Mom," Allison said.

Her mother didn't have to know.

How horrible. To be a mother and have to be this concerned about your child. Allison felt guilty. All her life she had tried to protect her mother from any unfortunate event.

"I didn't feel a thing," Allison said. Which, actually, was true. Watching the cameraman raise his arm and bring the vase down upon her head, she had felt completely outside herself. She hadn't even felt the impact. She had only registered the surprise of it all.

The glass shards of the vase had been green.

"I want to go home," she told Danny.

Was this really her Danny? The Asian doctor holding her hand? She was not even sure where her home was.

"I don't think I locked the front door," she said.

"It's okay," Danny said.

Allison nodded.

She had always been lucky, really.

There were people who bad things happened to. She was not one of them.

"I bought a house," she told Danny. "Near the beach. It's beautiful. It's all the way in North Carolina, but that was the reason I could afford it. You should come," she said. "We used to go to the beach, didn't we?"

In the summer. Danny would drive her down to the Jersey Shore. Sometimes Lori would come along.

Allison's head felt almost as if it was beating, pounding from the place the hole was, pumping all of her memories out. All of a sudden, she could picture her house near the ocean clearly. She remembered writing in a new notebook, sitting on the front porch.

Every morning, she'd noted down her plans for the day: a walk on the beach, then a swim. A turkey sandwich for lunch. Maybe again for dinner. Maybe with a salad. On some nights, she would open a bottle of wine. Every night, she slept in her own bed in her own house.

Allison appreciated the wonder of it all. For that week and a half, she'd been happy.

〰〰〰

Allison woke up, still in a hospital bed.

She was sitting up this time. She was actually strapped into the bed, restraints around her chest. For all she knew, she might be in a mental hospital. Still, she could not think of a reason this would happen. She was not suicidal. She was not crazy.

Was she crazy?

"Mom?" she called out. "Are you here? Mom?"

Allison's mother was not there.

She was all alone in the room, hooked up to even more machines, beeping and blinking, than before. This was a different room. The view from the window looked out onto her elementary school. She had taken note of this same view visiting her father. Did that mean she was on the seventh floor? Her father should have been on the cardiology floor, but they had done tests on his brain, so he had been with the neurology patients on the seventh floor. He had the same view in his room. It was surreal.

Allison wanted to scream, but her throat was dry.

"Mom?" she repeated. "Mommy?"

Allison always wanted her mother to help her. That was always her first thought. But then, when she was with her mother, she found herself irritable, wanted to be alone. It did not make sense to Allison. There was a button next to the bed, and Allison pressed it because that was how hospitals worked. She waited and she waited and she did not know if it was a long time or short. A nurse finally came into her room. Allison had never seen this nurse before. She wanted the Jamaican nurse back.

"Where is my mother?" Allison asked.

"She is going to be right back," this nurse told her. She was short, dark-skinned, Indian, or maybe Pakistani, wearing wire-rimmed glasses. She had pretty, straight hair pulled back into a ponytail. She looked nice. "She told me she had to walk her dog. She is going to be right back."

That made sense to Allison.

It also hurt her feelings.

Allison had no idea how long she had been in the hospital. A day. Maybe a week. Why was she still there? Why was she in this strange sitting-up position? She was wearing a blue hospital gown. She had a white plastic hospital bracelet around her wrist. It felt constricting. She tried to slip it off, but it was too tight. It would have to be cut off. She wanted the restraints off, too. Allison was officially a patient. How did she not remember any of this happening?

Allison did not know what to do next. Allison was going to scream. But then she didn't.

It would not be fair to the nurse. The nurse was nice. The nurse would take care of her. Nurses liked it when the patients, and the families of the patients, treated them with the respect they deserved. Kindness. Usually it was returned.

Allison wished she had not woken up alone like this. There had to be someone else if her mother was walking the dog. Her brother. Her brother could be there. Where was he?

He had a full-time job. He had a baby. He lived in Westchester. Of course he was not able to be there. He almost never visited their father when he was in the hospital, and their father had been dying.

"I don't like this," Allison said to the nurse, pointing at the restraints. "Why am I strapped in? Can you undo this? This makes me feel like I am a prisoner. Am I a prisoner?"

The nurse smiled at Allison. "Of course this must seem strange to you."

She undid the straps and lowered Allison's bed.

"Thank you," Allison said.

Allison's own voice sounded strange to her.

"We do this after brain surgery," the nurse said. "It's very common."

"What?" Allison said. "Brain surgery? I did not need brain surgery. Where is Danny?" she asked, remembering him as she said his name. Danny, her old friend. Was he really her doctor? They used to get drunk together. Danny had held her hair once while she threw up on the lawn on the way back from a party. He had written philosophy papers for her.

"Do you mean Dr. Yang?" the nurse asked. "I will page him. The doctor will want to know that you are awake."

"I am awake," Allison said.

At least she had not imagined him. Allison was not exactly sure what was real. Outside, in the hall, something had started to beep. It was a quiet, steady beep. Four beeps in a row and then the noise stopped. And then started again. It was almost worse that the beeping wasn't loud because Allison was not sure whether or not she was actually hearing it.

Allison watched the nurse looking at her chart, checking

numbers on the monitors. The nurse seemed completely calm. The nurse did not seem to be on the verge of insanity because of an intermittent beep in the hallway.

Allison had not always been the best when her father was sick, and it was because of all the noise in the hospital. It was constant. She had tried hard to ignore it. She would sit at her father's bedside and they would play gin rummy. They had watched an entire season of *Star Trek* that her father had never watched before on Allison's iPad. He had not even been aware that there was a new *Star Trek*. But sometimes, when the noise got to be too much, she would put on her noise-canceling headphones, and take them off only when her dad wanted to talk.

"Can you make that noise stop?" Allison asked now.

The nurse shook her head.

"You get used to it," she said.

Allison would not get used to it. She reached for the gooey spot on her head. There was a bandage covering it. She seemed to still have her hair. They had not shaved it off.

"I had brain surgery?"

"You did," the nurse said.

"Jesus," Allison said. "No one asked me first. I would have said no. I know that skulls can heal on their own. I know this."

She did not know how, but, somehow, she knew this.

The nurse with the pretty ponytail laughed. It was a kind laugh, not condescending, but that did not make it better. "You already had the surgery. You came through just fine. I am going to call Dr. Yang. I will call your mother, too. You have been sleeping for a very long time."

"So why was I sitting up like that?"

"To prevent swelling in your face."

"Terrific."

Allison was surprised by how angry she felt at this very nice nurse with the shiny ponytail. The nurse peered into her eyes with a miniature flashlight; it was something they seemed to do. It was extremely annoying. The nurse did not ask first.

"Follow the light with your eyes," she said.

Allison did this. It seemed stupid to argue.

"Your speech sounds fine," the nurse said. "That is a really good sign."

"I need some water," Allison said.

"I'll get you some water."

Allison was mad at her mother, mad at her mother for leaving her alone in the hospital, for letting her wake up alone like this. She was mad at her mother for taking her to the hospital in the first place.

The nurse poured water for Allison into a small plastic cup. She put a straw in the cup and Allison drank from it. The water was room temperature, tepid, disgusting. In her previous life, Allison had a fancy water bottle. It had a beautiful flower pattern on it. This water bottle kept the water crazy cold. Allison had never gotten over it, how cold the water stayed. She wanted to drink water like that now, cold and good. She wanted to drink water out of that flowered water bottle. She was afraid she had lost it. She had no idea where this water bottle was. In her car? In the cameraman's house?

The cameraman. Allison remembered the cameraman. He had hit her on the head. With a glass vase. He had seemed fine. He rode a bike, for Christ's sake. He had cats.

Allison could not remember the cameraman's name or how she came to be in his house. Why would she have stayed with him when she had a nice house of her own? It was not because he was attractive. She did not remember being lonely. She had liked being alone. She had just gotten away from a guy. Her memories were jumping all over the place.

Suddenly, she remembered the last episode of *Star Trek* she'd watched with her dad before he died. It was one with Ashley Judd, before she became famous.

"What a pretty girl," her dad had said.

Allison had agreed. She had always thought Ashley Judd was beautiful. Allison never would have predicted what would happen to Ashley Judd, the revelations made in her autobiography about her childhood, the stories about Harvey Weinstein. It made Allison incredibly sad for Ashley Judd, even though she had gone on to spark the Me Too movement, become a human rights ambassador, a genuine role model.

Brain surgery, Allison knew, was bad.

She had driven all the way from North Carolina, her brain wide open. Her mind really did feel jumbled. It had felt fine, before the hospital. Now she was confused.

What had they done to her?

Where was Danny Yang?

And why was he even here, after all the time they had not talked to each other?

Allison remembered. Danny was a doctor. Danny was her doctor. A brain surgeon. Maybe he had operated on *her* brain.

Danny would tell her the truth. Unless he was one of them now. Allison could feel herself growing upset, tears welling in her eyes. She became aware of a headache that spread all the way from the back of her skull to shoot rays of pain out of her ears and eyes.

And then, like a dream, her mother's friend Shelley walked into the room. Shelley Shapiro. Bringing flowers, pretty yellow and purple flowers. Irises. Allison had always liked Shelley. She used to be the mayor of Englewood. She had come to the hospital to visit Allison's father, too. Shelley had been in the room when her father died.

"Look at you," Shelley said. "You are awake. Your mother is going to be so happy."

"I'm fine," Allison said, blinking away the tears.

"Of course you are," Shelley said. "What a good girl you are."

~~~~

*A*llison had never been a sick person before.

She had always been the kind of person who took good health for granted. She would get irritated if she had a cold that lasted longer than a day. She had never broken a bone. Never gotten the flu.

It made Allison want to scream when her brain surgeon, the very professional Dr. Daniel Yang, explained to her what had happened to her, why they had to perform emergency surgery. He had already cut into her head, and without asking her first. There really couldn't be much worse than that.

And the truth was, Allison had trouble listening to him explain. She knew it was important, what he told her, that she might even be able to forgive him if she understood his reasons, but still, Allison did not listen. Allison did not know whether this was because she had had brain surgery or her mind wandered because that was just what her mind did. Allison had never paid great attention in class, or listened well when someone gave her directions after she had asked for them. She realized she might never know for sure again.

Really, nothing Danny said mattered. The surgery was done. She could look it up on the Internet or she could ask him again later, once she was able to focus. When there wasn't a persistent beeping coming from the machine behind the IV, a noise that no one besides Allison seemed to hear. She looked at Danny as he talked, studying how he had changed over the years, what was different. Danny was not balding, not exactly, but his hairline had definitely receded. He had not gained weight. He looked better older. He had always seemed like a little boy in college.

"Earth to Allison?" Danny said. "Are you listening?"

He knew she hadn't been, but it bothered her that he addressed her in this familiar way. He did not have the right to make assumptions about her.

Allison stared at him.

"It's okay," Danny said. "I know it's a lot."

Then he started over again, explaining what the surgery had accomplished, why it was necessary. Allison missed parts, again, closing her eyes, trying to block out the beeping, but she did hear him say that she had suffered a depressed skull fracture. While this often did not require surgery, her brain had swollen in a way that was troubling, and there was also fluid leakage that had to be contained. It could not wait.

And maybe, maybe that was true.

Allison wanted to believe him.

"That monitor is making a buzzing sound," Allison said, pointing to a piece of machinery.

"It is?" Danny said. "I don't hear a thing. I'm sorry if it's bothering you. Do you have any questions? About the procedure?"

"So you did not require my consent? You thought it was okay to operate without my consent."

"It's hospital policy to save our patients' lives, Allison," Dr. Daniel Yang said. "Aren't you glad we saved your life?"

Danny Yang looked confused. She had confused him in

college, too. Danny always had simple ideas about law and order, how the game of life worked.

"Unless there is a DNR," Allison said.

"Unless there is a DNR, I suppose," Danny agreed. "Do you have one?"

Allison shook her head. She would have to sign one after she got out of the hospital.

"Even if you had one," Danny said, "I would have performed this surgery. It was a simple procedure. And it was a success. Nothing unexpected, no complications. You are lucid. You are talking in full sentences. I expect that you are going to make a full recovery."

"Am I supposed to be grateful?" Allison said.

Allison did not know why she sounded so angry. Maybe it was because she was angry. She was furious. She did not understand, still, how she had ended up in this hospital bed. This was not where she was supposed to be.

She also felt embarrassed.

For being so much trouble.

For not being grateful.

She looked at the flowers Shelley had given her. For that, Allison was grateful. At least someone had thought to bring her flowers. Not her mother. Not her brain surgeon. But, mainly, she was angry. She was incredibly pissed off and did not know why.

Allison tried to touch the place where there was a hole in her head and touched the bandage.

"I would try to keep your hand off the bandage," Danny said. "You don't want to disturb the wound."

The wound, he said. That was what he called the hole in Allison's head.

"Do you have any questions?" Danny asked her. "I would be happy to answer questions. I want you to understand. We had to perform the surgery. There was no choice to be made."

Allison shook her head. "I might have questions later," she said. "It doesn't seem fair that you want me to ask them now."

"Okay," Danny said. "I am not going anywhere."

Allison stared at him.

They weren't friends. Not really. This was not how you rekindled a friendship. Danny had all the power. Allison could not make sense of it. He had saved her life and now she was angry at him.

Allison's mother did have questions, a long list, for Allison's doctor, which was what Danny was, but once again Allison failed to listen. Not to the questions. Not to the answers. She had already heard the important parts.

There were other doctors in the room, a group of them, actually, all of them standing by her bed holding clipboards. It was a teaching hospital, but Allison had not agreed to this, either, to function as a subject of their education. She wanted this group of doctors to leave. For her mother to leave. It was too loud in her room. Allison wanted to talk to Danny alone.

It was so weird that her doctor was Danny Yang.

She might have asked for a different brain surgeon, given a choice. It wasn't like he was a top student. He had struggled with organic chemistry.

Allison could not remember the last time she had seen him. Probably it was college graduation. She had not made an effort to talk to him that day. In fact, weird as it had felt, she had avoided him. It was clear they were going to go their own ways. Allison did not want to make small talk, or pretend that she was interested in keeping in touch. It had felt sad at the time. It felt sad now, looking at him, glad that he was there. She had not mistreated him. She had been honest. It was college. Now he stayed in her room after the other doctors left, just like she had hoped he would. She thought she could apologize to him, once they were alone.

Danny Yang.

She was glad he was there.

He had saved her life, maybe.

He had held her hand at her bedside.

He loved her.

"Mom," Allison said. "Do you remember Danny? Dr. Yang. This is Danny. We went to college together."

Allison's mother did not remember.

"We lived in the same dorm freshman year."

Allison's mother still looked confused. Allison was annoyed by this, and annoyed at herself, the way she was annoyed at *everyone*. Of course it was confusing.

Danny was wearing a white coat. Glasses. He did not used to wear glasses.

"You went to college together?"

"He used to drive me back to school sometimes," Allison said. "He's been in our house. He's from Tenafly."

Her mother had once made a comment about how the Tenafly schools used to be all Jewish, but now the Asians were taking over. That had seemed to Allison like an incredibly racist comment. Technically, though, Allison supposed, it was also true.

"You're that Danny?" her mother asked.

Poor eighteen-year-old Danny Yang. Probably everybody had treated him badly.

"What are the chances, of all the doctors in the world, that you would be Allison's?"

"Her brain surgeon, no less," Danny said.

"That is so impressive," Allison's mother said. "You're a brain surgeon. Your mother must be so proud."

"I didn't actually need surgery." Allison could not let this go. "I was fine."

Danny Yang, of course, had probably just explained the contrary with that emergency-surgery speech. He smiled, kindly, at Allison. He did not seem to be a pompous asshole, which was her experience with most doctors. Her father's doctor. She did not know what to think about her own doctor, Danny Yang. She kept going back and forth.

"You needed the surgery, Allison," he said. "There was swelling in your brain that could have killed you. And the operation went well. Really well. Brain surgery sounds much scarier than it is. You are going to get out of here in a few days. Better than ever."

Allison reached up to touch her bandage. The top of her head itched. She also wanted to press down, feel the gooey spot. Somehow, then, maybe it would make sense to her.

"Stop it," her mother said.

"Your mother is right. You should try to keep your hands off the bandage," Danny said. "You don't want to disturb the stitches."

"You didn't leave anything?" she said.

"In your brain?" Danny said. "Like a scalpel? Or a pen?"

Allison hesitated. She was not going to ask, but then he did. It was the one question she had. "Maybe a bug could have flown into my brain? A small one. Gotten stuck in the soft tissue. I know it sounds crazy. But I feel this itch. And I hear a buzzing."

Allison did not want to, but she could not help herself, and she scratched at her head.

"No," he said. "No bugs."

Allison appreciated that he was taking her seriously. The roles in their relationship seemed to have switched. Allison used to be the one in charge.

"I didn't leave a bug in your brain. I promise you," Danny said.

"The itch."

"You just had brain surgery. I think you are going to feel a lot of things. Some confusion. Headaches. Discomfort. Some memory loss, even. In the very beginning. An itch doesn't trouble me."

"Are you sure?" Allison asked.

Because Allison was still not sure whether she could trust him. Allison did not trust doctors. Her father had been killed by his doctors. A whole array of doctors, in fact. They had misdiagnosed him. Waited far too long to treat him and then had not been aggressive enough.

Her doctor, Danny, had been aggressive, which was just as bad.

"Allison," Danny said, and then he touched her face, unconcerned that Allison's mother was also in the room. He reached out for her hand and did not let go. "This is definitely not how I wanted to see you again," he said. "But I am very, very glad to see you."

Allison nodded.

She was glad to see him again, too, but she didn't have

the words. She was tired, drifting off to sleep despite herself. Knowing that Danny was at her bedside, watching her sleep. He had had his hands inside her brain.

The last thing she saw was an image on the inside of her eyelids, an orange and white cat sleeping on a white bedspread. It was purring, but the purring was not a noise that upset her. She reached out to pet the cat, but the cat jumped off the bed, leaving her abandoned once more.

〰〰〰

Allison awoke to find two police officers in her room. Two tall men, standing over her bed, wearing uniforms. Allison screamed.

She checked to see whether the men were holding vases. Vases. That seemed so crazy to her. But then Allison remembered. She had been hit with a vase. Whereas police officers carried guns. She had never trusted police officers.

The nurse, the one with the shiny ponytail, rushed into her room. "It's okay, it's okay." She told Allison that it was fine. They were there to help her. They had been called because of the glass pieces found in her hair. This was protocol when an assault victim was brought into the hospital.

"Am I in danger?" Allison asked.

The nurse blinked. She did not seem to understand the question. This made Allison feel sad. Even when she was there with her dad, she had this idea that the nurses could be her friends, but that was not exactly right, either. They were doing their job, and part of their job was to be kind. "No," the nurse said. "These men are here to help you."

The police officers wanted to know what had happened to Allison.

"Where is my mom?" Allison asked.

It was funny how whenever she felt unsure, threatened, that was always Allison's first thought. She wondered why her mother wasn't in the room now. Probably she was walking the dog. Gibson was on a new medication and needed to pee all the time. Her mother could not be in the hospital around the clock. Somehow her mother was never there when Allison wanted her, but that wasn't her mother's fault.

Allison did not want to talk to the police.

What was done was done.

On TV, there was usually a policewoman at the bedside in a female victim's hospital room. Allison wondered why she hadn't been sent one of them. She wanted her nurse back, too. The one who called her honey, in her beautiful Jamaican accent. She hadn't seen that nurse since her first day.

"You woke me up," Allison told the police officers.

It was so hard to sleep in the hospital.

Allison heard the accusation in her voice. This was wrong, of course. Talking this way to the police, dangerous people to act angry at. And maybe they were even there to help her.

But they had woken Allison up, and she needed her sleep. All she wanted to do was sleep, but it felt impossible. There was always some machine beeping. The nurses were nice, but they woke her up, too, checking her blood pressure, changing an IV, making her take medicine. This was crazy. How was she supposed to get better?

Allison had a roommate on the other side of a screen, and this roommate watched TV nonstop. Reality shows, game shows, Fox News. The roommate refused to turn it down. She'd yelled at Allison, even, saying that she was paying for the hospital and could watch the TV as loud as she wanted to. Allison did not dare disagree. Instead, Allison started to cry, because she hated to be yelled at.

And then there was a small woman who woke Allison up to take her meal order, food that Allison would not eat. Being in the hospital was Allison's worst nightmare. Drawn out. Belittling. Never-ending. It seemed so unfair that her father had had to die here. Allison found herself constantly apologizing to her father, wanting to go back in time.

Now Allison stared at the police officers by her bed, looking at their badges, as if that would make it better. They were large men. One black, one white, like in a buddy movie. One of the police officers showed Allison a picture of the hole in her head, the glass pieces, the soft tissue around her brain. Allison asked to hold the phone and looked at the picture, almost mesmerized.

Most people never got to see the insides of their head.

"Can you send me this?" she asked.

"You want this?" one asked.

"I do," she said. She gave him her email address.

"We just want to ask you some questions about how this happened," the other police officer said. "Who did this to you?"

Allison did not want to answer any questions.

"Can I have my lawyer present?" she asked.

Allison did not, of course, have a lawyer. This was a line from a television show, something a person would ask after being arrested. Allison did not know why she would be placed under arrest, but it seemed like the right thing to say.

At that moment, Danny came into the room in his white doctor's coat.

Allison smiled at him, grateful.

"I don't think that's necessary," one of the police officers said. "We're here to help you. You aren't in any kind of trouble."

"I'm not?" Allison asked.

"Hell no," said the other officer.

Allison understood that she was supposed to laugh, but she did not laugh.

"Can I have my doctor with me?" Allison asked.

Danny Yang held her hand while the police questioned her. Allison squeezed it. For the time being, she was done being angry with him. She allowed herself the right to feel angry again later. For now, he was there and she needed him.

It felt wrong to need a man at this juncture in her life, when it was a man, after all, who had put her in this hospital bed. Allison knew her friend Lori would tell her to cut the crap with the feminist bullshit, just accept this kindness. Allison had not talked to Lori. Lori probably did not even know that she was here.

Danny nodded at Allison.

"It's okay," he said. "They want to help you. You can talk to them."

"You'll stay? Please?"

"Of course I'll stay."

The nurse with the ponytail seemed surprised.

"Don't you have rounds?" she asked, looking at her watch.

"I have time," Danny said. "If my patient wants me here, I am staying."

"Is that okay?" the nurse asked Allison, looking down at their hands, which were entwined. "Are you sure? Is this okay?"

Allison nodded.

"It's fine," Allison said. "I want him to stay."

The only redeeming part of being in the hospital was visits from Danny. She had been there for four days, and he was her most regular visitor. He was already at the hospital. It was easy for him to pop by. Most times, he would bring pudding.

Allison used to bring her father chocolate pudding. Rice pudding, too. Allison was not, herself, a fan of rice pudding. She did not like vanilla, either. Only chocolate. Allison loved chocolate pudding.

"We are old friends," she told the nurse. "From college."

"You should have talked to me before questioning my patient," Danny said to the police. "She is recovering from a traumatic head injury."

"I am?" Allison was surprised.

This sounded serious. But he had told her she was fine. She felt fine. She wanted to go home. But the hospital would not let her.

"Can we ask your patient some questions?" the police officer asked Danny. Allison could almost hear the police officer rolling his eyes.

"Is that okay with you?" Danny asked Allison.

"Not really," she said. "I want them to leave. They have already been asking me questions."

"I think you should help them," Danny said. "You were assaulted, Allie. I removed shards of glass from the tissue of your brain. I think we should catch the creep who did this to you."

Allison looked at Danny, surprised.

Allison had thought that what had happened to her

was private. Her own personal story. But now other people seemed to know.

It seemed harder not to talk to the police officers than to give in, so Allison did. Holding Danny's hand, Allison told them all she could remember.

Allison told them about the interview on local television. The glass vase. She was able to describe the cameraman's appearance. She did not know the cameraman's last name.

"I hate the name Keith," she told them.

"I should have known better," she added.

The police officers did not disagree.

She wished they had.

That made sense, though.

It was always the woman's fault.

Allison had not, for instance, been forced to go back with the cameraman to his house. She did not have to kiss him. Allison did not want to talk about this in front of Danny. It was mortifying. He would stop loving her. And that did not seem fair.

The police, Danny, probably the whole world, would blame her if they knew she had engaged in sexual activity with the cameraman voluntarily. Allison also did not want to talk about this because it did not matter, anyway.

The past was past.

She was alive.

She would never go back to North Carolina. The beach was nice, but it was not the place for her. Forget about hurricanes. Even her next-door neighbor had proven himself to be menacing.

And there were beaches closer by. Beaches in New Jersey.

Asbury Park, where there was good coffee and Korean fusion tacos on the boardwalk.

Still, the police did not go away. They kept on asking her questions.

No, she did not know the address of the cameraman's house.

"He had two cats," she told them.

No, she did not remember the name of the TV station he worked for.

"I had a beach house," she told the police.

Sometimes it seemed to Allison that the whole house thing was just something she had dreamed. She was not even sure she had taken a picture of it.

"It was blue. My house. A hurricane blew it down like it was made of sticks." Allison looked at Danny. "Like the Three Little Pigs. It was such a pretty house. I did not want to spend another night at the motel," she said. "And he seemed nice." She could feel tears form in her eyes.

She realized how she sounded. *He seemed nice?* What a bad decision she had made. She had heard the saying *Don't blame the victim.* But even she blamed herself. Honestly, it was her fault. She had been stupid.

No, Allison did not remember the color of the cameraman's house. No, she did not know the answers to most of the rest of their questions. She had started to cry and still the police officers kept asking the questions.

"I want to stop," Allison said. "I'm tired."

Danny asked them to stop.

"My patient is tired," Danny said. "There can only be so many local TV stations in North Carolina. Only so many balding cameramen. That has to be plenty to go on. If you have more questions, you can come back later, after my patient has rested."

And then they were done. The officers said they would be giving all this information to the North Carolina police. Allison might hear from them, too.

"Fine," Allison said.

She would just not answer the phone if she saw a North Carolina area code.

That was easy.

That felt better.

"You'll find the guy, right?" Danny asked. "Lock the bastard up?"

It was curious, to Allison, how upset Danny was on her behalf. He seemed more upset than Allison was herself. She wished that she felt more.

Allison did not want justice done. She wanted to go home. And then she remembered. She did not have a home. And she did not want to rebuild her house. There would be another hurricane. And then another.

Before leaving the room, one of the police officers gave Allison his card. His name was Keith Montgomery.

Keith. It really was not that common a name. It was funny, really. Allison did not laugh. Of course, she could not trust this police officer. But she had known that from the outset.

Allison did not think that men who clearly believed her to be an idiot could be of use to her. Experience had already told her this much.

The first Keith had seemed too good to be true. He had been incredibly romantic. Flowers, chocolate, sex in the swimming pool. Though now that Allison thought about it, in the swimming pool all she really liked to do was swim.

"I'm glad they're gone," Allison told Danny.

"They just want to help you," Danny said.

Allison opened the chocolate pudding Danny had brought. She did not believe the police were there to help her. They wanted to solve a case. That was an entirely different thing.

Allison proceeded to eat the chocolate pudding. It was creamy and good, the only thing she felt like eating. She did not eat the hospital meals. One night her mother had been in the room when dinner was delivered. Her mother had eaten her chicken and then her dessert, a spongy pound cake. Her mother ate the overcooked green beans, too. It was weird, and Allison worried that her mother wasn't taking care of herself. What was she eating at home for dinner? Probably scrambled eggs and toast.

"Do you have any more of this?" Allison asked Danny.

"I do, actually," Danny said. He took one, then another, and then another pudding out of his pocket. It seemed as though he had planned this for dramatic affect.

"You were holding out on me," Allison said, laughing.

Danny laughed, too. "I just forgot about them."

There was something wonderful about the way Danny Yang was always at the hospital, always dropping by her room. He had come into her room once in the middle of the night, sure that she was asleep, but Allison could not sleep through the night in the hospital room.

Allison had been watching an episode of *Fleabag* on her phone. Danny had never heard of the show. It was strangely uncomfortable, sitting next to Danny, watching the main character have sex with a man she had met on a bus. Danny fidgeted and then he looked away. This could have told Allison everything she needed to know.

If she had not already known it, of course.

It was complicated, having your brain surgeon in love with you, but it also made the experience better. The anger she felt toward him was gone. Allison looked forward to seeing Danny. She felt better every time he came into her room.

Allison was not, however, in love with her brain surgeon. Or, she did not want to be. Danny had failed, no matter what he might think about himself.

Part Three

*C*oming home.

It was a do-over.

Allison was all bandaged up, no more hole in her head.

Except, really, it would always be there.

This time, Allison was returning from the hospital. She was in the passenger seat. Her mother drove, Shelley Shapiro in the back, holding a fresh bouquet of flowers.

Back at the house, Gibson barked excitedly, and Allison sat on the bottom step in the kitchen and petted her mother's dog. She was doing it all over.

"Good dog," Allison said. "I love you. Good boy."

Allison went to the bathroom and took a Xanax and then, after a moment's hesitation, a Percocet. Her head hurt. She had told Danny she would not need these prescriptions when he gave them to her, but she had been wrong.

Allison's mother took the flowers that Shelley had gotten for her homecoming and cut them, putting them into a different vase. Her mother seemed nervous. Allison could not remember exactly what had happened the first time she came home, but she still had a bruise on her arm from when her mother punched her in the car. Allison did not remember this happening, but her mother told her about it. Her mother repeated the story in the kitchen as she arranged the flowers. About how scared she had been.

"I'm sorry, Mom," Allison said.

"You have to stop telling me how sorry you are," her mother responded. There was a sharpness to her tone, and somehow this comment stung.

Allison wanted to ask her mother to be nice to her but decided it was better to say nothing. She had decided after the death of her father that she would not fight with her mother ever again. She had not anticipated brain surgery.

Shelley kissed Allison on the cheek. "I'm going to go," she said. "You need to get settled."

Shelley hugged her mother. She promised to come back later. Shelley was almost ninety years old. It seemed crazy that this woman was doing so much to help them.

"You get some sleep," she told Allison.

That was what Allison wanted to do.

Allison watched as Shelley pulled out of their driveway, and then as an enormous white SUV pulled into the driveway. She would not be able to crawl into her childhood bed and pull the covers over her head. Not just yet. It was her brother, Adam, who had not come to see her in the hospital. Of course, he was here now.

Adam had come with his family. His beautiful wife, Ava. Their baby, the one Allison had never met. This was the day she was going to meet the baby. It felt like a little bit too much. Maybe a lot too much. She did not see why he had to come that day. Why he had not come to the hospital, where a guest might have been welcome.

"I wish your brother didn't have to come today," her mother said. "It's too much."

Allison agreed. Those were her very thoughts, but this was what Adam wanted to do. This was what fit into his schedule. Her brother did what he wanted to do. He always had. Firstborn son. As if it was his birthright.

From the kitchen window, Allison watched him getting out of the car and opening the door to the backseat. He emerged with a car seat covered with a blue baby blanket and, under the blanket, Allison assumed, the baby. The baby. Still a baby.

Adam's wife got out of the car. Ava, tall and blond, just as she had been the last time. Adam and Ava spent a long time beside the car talking to each other, whispering, saying things they obviously did not feel comfortable saying in the house. It appeared to be a minor argument.

"The baby won't be interesting until he is six months," Allison's mother said to Allison. "Then I will love and play with the baby. I have told Adam that."

Allison nodded. She had heard this before. The baby was currently five months old, so that time was coming soon. Or it was also a long time off, depending on your point of view. Allison had never heard another grandparent say something like that about a baby. A timeline for when she would love it. Grandparents were supposed to be crazy about babies from the moment they were born. She could imagine that Adam would be unhappy about this.

Her mother went to the door to greet them, giving kisses all around, to Adam and Ava, a beautiful couple, and admiring the baby. All Allison could see was a little face, the baby otherwise covered by a blanket. But it was a very cute little face. A perfectly shaped head. Wisps of blond hair. Blue eyes.

Ava was wearing running clothes. It seemed like she had barely gotten into the house, kissing Allison on the cheek, asking her how she was, and then beginning to stretch, before Allison could even formulate an answer.

Allison did not know how she was. The easiest answer, of course, was fine.

Ava, she was limber in a way Allison had never been. Ava did a forward bend, placed the palms of her hands on the floor, and stayed there, bent in half, for what seemed like a very long time. Allison was impressed.

They seemed like a perfect couple, Adam and Ava. They had alliteration going for them in their names, though it used to be Allison and Adam's alliteration, sister and brother. Adam and Ava were both lawyers. Somehow they both seemed better looking since the last time she had seen them. Ava was closer to Allison's age, but they never had anything in common. Now Ava—and Adam—had this seemingly perfect baby. Allison wondered why, then, her brother looked so angry. He had it all. Successful lawyer. Beautiful wife. Beautiful baby. Beautiful house. It felt, to Allison, as if perhaps Allison and her mother and the neurotic Gibson did not somehow meet his expectations. Yet they were the only family he had, so there he was.

"Seriously, how are you, Allison?" Ava repeated. "I was so upset when I heard about what happened to you."

"Me, too," Allison finally answered. "Really upset."

It occurred to Allison that her brother and sister-in-law could have at least sent flowers. If they were genuinely upset. Perhaps they did not think Allison was the type of person to appreciate flowers, but she did.

"Allison." Adam scowled at her.

Okay, so it appeared that less than a minute into their visit, Allison had been rude to Ava. This had not been her intention. She needed to answer the question in a manner that could not be construed as sarcastic. How was she? Allison wondered.

How was she?

How was she? How was she? How was she?

Allison felt tears form in her eyes. She did not know how to answer. Even how to come up with an honest answer she might be willing to share with Ava. Allison did not know. How she was. It was crazy. The tears started streaming from her eyes. She was crying, again, for no reason. Danny had told her that this could happen. She was going to be one hundred percent sometime soon, but "soon" was open-ended. It did not mean, for instance, within the next fifteen minutes. What was soon? When would it stop? The headaches and the memory loss and the confusion and the crying?

Besides that, she was fine. Should she tell that to Ava? She did not want to have this conversation, but she imagined this would be what everyone would want to know.

Allison's mother handed her a tissue. Allison dried her face. The tears had stopped just as quickly as they'd come.

"I'm fine," she told Ava. She smiled a fake smile. "I have my health."

Ava squinted her eyes, wondering if it was a joke.

It *was* a joke.

It also wasn't a joke.

Allison wasn't sure whether Ava had a sense of humor.

This was not an answer to the question that her brother would find acceptable, but when did he ever find anything about Allison acceptable?

"You look fine," Ava said. "I could give you the name of my hairdresser if you want. She's a genius."

Allison's mouth dropped open.

Ava was serious, talking to Allison about her hair. Allison had not thought about it. True, she would have to do something about her hair. She would have to talk to a hairdresser, and the hairdresser would want to know how Allison was. But not right now.

It was off the charts, how much Allison did not want to see her brother or his wife right now.

"Sure," Allison said. "That would be great."

Allison was pleased with herself, anyway. She had given a polite answer to her sister-in-law.

Allison was trying.

"You're going for a run?" Allison's mother asked Ava. "You just got here."

Ava had not stopped stretching. The visit was only just beginning. Allison wondered how many hours they would stay. Soon, she could say that she needed to take a nap. She had just had brain surgery. So that might even be true.

Adam had set the car seat, with the baby, on the kitchen table. Allison looked at this baby. Her nephew. His eyes were blue, though Allison had heard that that could change. The baby looked at Allison and he smiled. He smiled! Allison held out her finger and the baby grabbed it. This, it appeared, was a baby that Allison very much wanted to meet. Allison was glad about this. It was not too late. She could tell her brother this, but it would also be better not to. Better to talk as little as possible. Better not to say anything wrong. Allison smiled, a big smile, back at the baby. She was already in love.

"I love you," Allison said to the baby.

Her brother heard this. He looked pleased. Allison felt pleased. Like a tightness in her chest had released.

"I like to run before I eat," Ava explained to her mother. "And I am hungry. Breast-feeding makes me ravenous. I won't be gone long. We'll catch up then. It's crazy, this motherhood business."

"Have a good run," Allison said.

That would be better, really, one less person she had to talk to.

"I'm really glad you're okay," Ava said. "I didn't realize how serious it was. Are you sure?"

Allison nodded.

She would not cry again.

"It's fine. I'm going to play with the baby."

Ava smiled, uncertain.

A peace had been reached, but it was ridiculous how quickly things had gone off the rails. There were all these rules in life, how you were supposed to behave. How you were supposed to make conversation. Her mother was supposed to love babies, but it turned out that she loved only babies six months and older. While her brother must certainly have been mad about that, he did not express this anger to their mother. He followed the rules. He kept his angry thoughts to himself.

Anyway, it was a beautiful day. Still summer. If Allison were a runner she would have wanted to go for a run, too.

Allison did not know the actual date. Allison had luxuriated in the fresh air, in the moments it had taken, leaving the hospital, to get into the car, and then from the car into her mother's house.

All of the tension in the room seemed to disappear. Then the beautiful baby in the car seat started to cry. The crying, unfortunately, was loud. Allison knew this about babies, but still the noise upset her.

This was all really too much, too soon. Her brother, fortunately, picked the baby up out of his car seat and cradled him in his arms. Almost like magic, the baby stopped crying. And it was nice to see the whole baby, out of his car seat. There he was, wearing the organic onesie Allison had sent them after he was born. It had blue dolphins on it and it had been expensive. French. The movie producer had told her where to buy it.

Adam gave the baby a bottle of milk and the baby drank it.

"It's breast milk," he said. "Ava pumped this morning."

"That's really wonderful," Allison's mother said. "I breast-fed until you were both a year old."

Allison nodded. Did her brother think she cared about the milk in the baby's bottle? Allison stared at the baby intently drinking breast milk from a bottle. Allison realized she had forgotten the baby's name.

Allison had forgotten a lot of things since the brain surgery. Danny had told her this was common. He had told her not to worry. He, of course, was not the one forgetting things.

"I don't like it," she had told him.

This was an understatement.

"I know," he'd said. "It will go away."

"How do you know?"

"I know," he'd said, which was a useless answer.

"When?"

"I don't know," Danny had told her. "It varies."

"That is a useless answer," Allison had said. "All of your answers are useless. Are you better with your other patients?"

Danny had shrugged, his feelings clearly hurt. It sucked, hurting your brain surgeon's feelings. It was also his fault, always making his feelings so apparent. Allison would never talk that way to a brain surgeon who was not in love with her.

Part of Allison was still back in the hospital, waiting for Danny to come with chocolate pudding, waiting for the next machine to start beeping. Part of Allison was also back on the beach, gazing at the waves, glad to be alive.

~~~~~

Allison watched the baby drink the milk, concentration all over his little face.

Adam was good with the baby.

Allison wished she could remember the baby's name.

She closed her eyes and tried to remember.

For no apparent reason, Gibson started to bark.

"Oh, Gibson," her mother said. "He is jealous about the baby. You have to pet the dog, Allison."

Allison petted the dog.

She looked at her brother and realized that he was talking to her, had been trying to maintain a conversation while feeding the baby, while Gibson continued to bark because he was jealous. Allison wondered what it was that could possibly be worth talking about.

Allison was confused.

She could not remember why she was in her mother's house. It was not Thanksgiving.

"What?" Allison asked her brother.

"I wanted to know if you want to hold the baby?"

Allison nodded. She did. She did want to hold the baby. She wanted to cradle something in her arms. Hold it close. Her brother placed the baby in Allison's arms, and she wanted to ask what his name was but knew that would get her in trouble. Allison would wait and listen, and someone would say the baby's name and it would be all right.

The baby, Allison decided, that was why Allison was there, in her mother's house. She was there to see the baby. He was five months old. It was high time. That made sense. She was there for a visit. This made her feel better.

Allison looked down at the baby's face. He seemed to have fallen back asleep. That seemed fast. He had only just woken up.

"Little baby," Allison murmured.

The baby felt good in her arms. Allison kissed the top of the baby's head.

"Milk coma," her brother said.

Allison nodded.

Allison wondered about her return ticket, how long she had booked this trip for, when she would be going back to LA. And then she remembered that she did not live in LA anymore. It was so fucking confusing. She had broken up with the movie producer, but she'd woken up that morning in a hospital bed, sad, wondering why he had not called, and then Danny came into her room, talking much too loudly.

"Big day," Danny had said, an enormous smile plastered on his face. "Going home." And Allison had smiled back at him, though she felt more disturbed than anything, realizing that she wasn't going back to Los Angeles. Sure, it was phony there and the traffic was awful, but she had also loved it. The sunshine. The beach. The hiking trails. The movie producer's swimming pool. She was not going back there. She could not remember why they had broken up, even.

She wanted to go back.

Back in time.

"He likes you," her brother said.

Allison gently cradled the baby, glad for the weight of this baby in her arms.

"I like him, too."

Allison looked at the baby. She had never thought that a baby could be calming.

"You really do look okay, Allie," her brother said, sitting across from her at the kitchen table. "I thought your whole head would have been shaved. I was kind of nervous, actually."

"You were nervous about how I would look?" Allison asked. "Is that why you didn't come to the hospital?"

Somehow, Allison still had most of her hair, though they had shaved the area where the surgery had taken place, leaving a strange bald spot. Allison almost wished her entire head had been shaved, because her hair didn't fall right anymore. She supposed she would have to do something about this. Maybe she would call Ava's hairdresser, but probably she wouldn't.

"We have just been really busy," Adam said. "Work. The baby. You were in and out really before we could make the trip."

Allison had been in the hospital for five days. It had felt like forever.

~~~~~

llison had had strange dreams in the hospital. She had dreamed about her father. They were taking a road trip. He was driving, speeding, telling her that in heaven there was as much shrimp as you could eat, when they heard a police siren. "That can't be for me," her father said. "In heaven, you can speed as much as you like." The siren got louder and Allison woke up.

This dream did not mean anything, except that she missed him. Why, she wondered, was he talking about shrimp?

"Allison?" her mother asked. She actually shook her by her shoulders. There was fear in her voice. "Are you okay?"

"Yeah," Allison said. "Sure. Of course I am. Why? Why did you shake me?"

"It looks like you went away for a second."

Allison had gone away, but she was not going to tell her mother that. Her mother and brother were talking about politics, and Allison was not up for that. She wanted to have a list, really, of subjects that she did not want to talk about.

"It's good to be a baby," Allison told the baby sleeping in her arms. Somehow, she was still holding the baby.

"He really is a good baby," her mother said.

No one had said the baby's name.

"What happened to the guy that did this to you?" Adam asked her. "Did you press charges?"

This, of course, was high up on the do-not-discuss list.

"Adam?" Allison said, not sure what else to say, because this was none of his business. It was just conversation for him, but it was her life. It was private. He had no right.

"The police have to catch him first," Allison's mother said. Her mother, too. They all thought that they could talk about her as if she wasn't sitting there.

"What is going on with that?" Adam asked. "Do the police have any leads?"

The baby woke up, started to cry again, and Allison was glad. Glad the baby was awake. Glad that she had something to do. The conversation would shift, would shift back to the baby. She stood up, started walking around the kitchen.

"Look," she said to the baby. "That is the refrigerator. Inside, it's full of food. That is your dad, that's Adam, he is my older brother. That is your grandmother. That is a bowl full of apples on the table. I love apples. Do you like apples?"

"He's too small to like apples," Adam said. "No teeth."

Allison frowned at her brother. She continued her tour of the kitchen. "You will get bigger and you will love apples."

"He can start with applesauce," Allison's mother said.

Allison nodded. Of course, this was true. This was the kind of conversation she wanted to have. The baby seemed to appreciate Allison's tour of the kitchen. He had stopped crying. "You are going to love applesauce," she said. "You don't need to have any teeth. It just slides down."

Adam nodded. "That's true."

"These are flowers," Allison said. "Shelley brought me

these flowers this morning. Someday, you will meet Shelley. She is honorary family, really. You will love Shelley."

"Shelley is going to come back later today," Allison's mother said. "She wants to meet the baby."

Again, her mother called the baby the baby. Maybe the baby did not have a name after all.

"Shelley is going to come later today," Allison repeated back to the baby. "She is going to love you, too, little baby."

The baby felt wonderful in her arms. Even the walking felt good. Danny had encouraged her to walk more in the hospital, but Allison had not wanted to leave her room, did not like the hospital hallways, seeing other sick people. The families of sick people. The beeping.

Allison looked down and smiled at the baby, and the baby smiled back at her. The baby was like a smiling machine.

Allison continued to walk.

"Hi, baby," Allison said. It did not even matter that she did not remember the baby's name. Her brother had not seemed to notice. "Little baby." Allison kissed the top of the baby's head.

Adam walked over to the refrigerator.

"There's nothing to eat, Mom," he said after a while.

He started putting rotten food on the kitchen table. A full container of strawberries that had grown moldy. A wilted lettuce. "This yogurt expired last month."

"It's still good," her mother said. "You just have to smell it first. The expiration date is just for when a store can sell it."

Adam put an old sour cream on the table. An almost empty jar of mustard. All of this food was, in fact, rotten, but it did not feel kind to point this out to their mother. Allison wished that he would stop. This was nothing new, anyway. There was rarely food in their mother's refrigerator. She wished that he would sit back down. He was making Allison uncomfortable, worried that he would upset their mother.

"I thought we would order in," her mother said. "We can get turkey sandwiches. I meant to get to the store, but I have been so busy getting everything ready for Allison."

This was actually true.

Her mother, for instance, had gone to the pharmacy to fill Allison's prescriptions. She had gone to the hospital every day, even though it was the same place where her husband had died, even if she hadn't been in the room during the moments when Allison had wanted her.

Besides that, there *was* food.

Her mother had picked up Entenmann's powdered doughnuts at the drugstore that morning. Allison did not particularly like this kind of doughnut, but it was fine. She appreciated the gesture. Her mother was exhausted and it was Allison's fault, having frightened her mother, having passed out in her car, having had brain surgery. Allison felt guilty about all of this.

"There are some doughnuts on the table," Allison told her brother, and her brother seemed surprisingly placated by this. He sat back down and their mother brought him a doughnut.

Allison shook her head no.

The baby made a noise, a watery squishing sound, and an unpleasant smell filled the kitchen.

"Can you change him?" Adam asked Allison.

Allison blinked.

"I'm eating a doughnut," Adam said. "I just need a second."

"Um, Adam," she said. "I just had brain surgery."

Allison was not changing diapers. She had just had brain surgery. Allison handed the baby back to her brother and, despite the smell, he did not get up until he had finished his doughnut. When he was done, and only then, he got up and took the baby into the downstairs bathroom to change the diaper. Allison went to the upstairs bathroom, where she took another Percocet.

It was, Allison knew, early in the day, but this was also her first day out. Allison was surprised that she fought with her adult brother. She had adored him as a child. She did not know when everything had changed.

Allison looked at herself in the mirror.

Her hair was greasy and it was uneven, shaved around the hole in her head. She would have to get a haircut. Probably, she should cut it all off. Allison loved her hair. Long and brown and wavy and thick.

It was also just hair.

It would grow back.

"Hi, Allison," she said.

She was alive.

It was not the end of the world, being back in New Jersey.

Another pill had been a good idea. Almost right away, she felt better. Floaty.

It did not even matter that Adam had put the freshly changed baby back into her arms when she returned to the kitchen and then wandered away to watch TV in the living room. Ava somehow had not returned from her run. She must run for a really long time.

Really, it was fine for Allison to be in the kitchen with her mother and the baby and Gibson. The dog was sitting in her mother's lap. The dog was her mother's baby. They sat in companionable silence. Everything would be fine, Allison thought, if she were not required to speak.

She stroked the baby's hair.

Allison had thought she would feel nothing for the baby, but, instead, something had melted inside of her. The baby had soft hair. Little toes. Little fingers. Big eyes. An intelligent expression. A heart-stopping smile. He squeezed Allison's fingers.

I could have one of you, Allison thought.

"Phoebe," Allison whispered, kissing the top of the baby's hair, because if she had a baby, and if the baby was a girl, that was what she would name her. She could pretend that this baby was a girl. There was no harm in that. "Phoebe."

The doorbell rang.

Her mother had the dog on her lap and so Allison got up to answer it, still holding baby Phoebe. Allison was not surprised that Shelley would come back so soon. Maybe she even brought food, lunch for everyone, and then her mother would not have to go out for it. Allison opened the door, and she even said, "Shelley!"

But it was Danny, Danny Yang, wearing his white doctor's coat. Danny had been to her house before, years ago, back in college. Still, she was surprised to see him.

"I was on my way home," he said. "And I thought I would stop by. I hope that's okay. It's hard. The transition from the hospital, no matter how happy you are to leave. I just wanted to see how you were."

Allison's heart did a little flutter, the way it did every time he came into her room at the hospital.

"Who is this that you are holding?" he asked.

"This is Phoebe," Allison told Danny. "My niece."

Danny smiled at Allison, and then he leaned over the baby's head, and then, they kissed.

Allison did not remember this, Danny being a good kisser in college. They grinned at each other. Allison felt inexplicably happy.

"Hello, Phoebe," he said.

~~~~~~

Part
Four

Danny Yang had a swimming pool on the roof of his apartment building. Allison had not been expecting this, but she felt enormously lucky. It was a beautiful swimming pool. Allison was sure that she would not have moved in with the movie producer if he had not had a pool. She had a weakness for swimming pools the way some people need to pet every dog they see.

Danny Yang's building was in Fort Lee, New Jersey, of all places, a place Allison had never considered a legitimate place to live. He lived in one of two luxury skyscrapers that towered over every other building in the area.

Allison could remember being in the car with her parents, sitting in the backseat on the way to New York City to see a Broadway show, and her father commenting on the construction. "Who," he wanted to know, "would ever want to live there?"

The answer, it turned out, was Danny Yang.

Danny said it was only a fifteen-minute commute from the hospital.

And the pool, it was nice. It was really nice. A tiled lap pool with an incredible view of New York City from the roof.

Allison could see the Hudson River, the George Washington Bridge, the long row of trees lining the Henry Hudson Parkway all the way downtown to the Freedom Tower.

"Nice, huh?" Danny said.

"Yeah," Allison said.

It was.

She felt strangely at peace.

This was not a ramshackle blue house in North Carolina two blocks away from the ocean. It was not a super-hip, modern house in Silver Lake. But it was pretty good.

The apartment itself was fine, new and modern and clean, but it was the pool on the roof that was the reason to live there. It was surprisingly quiet up on the roof. It was heavenly quiet. Almost nowhere was it as quiet as it was up on this roof. Allison felt as close to the clouds as she had ever been.

Two days after she had been released from the hospital, Danny had picked her up at her mother's house and brought her over, telling her to bring a bathing suit.

"You still like to swim, don't you?" he asked Allison as they drove.

Allison smiled.

They had taken beach trips together in college. Driving in his father's BMW convertible down to the Jersey Shore. They would get drunk in bars in Asbury Park. Sometimes they would take Allison's friend Lori.

"Of course I still like to swim," Allison said. "It's not like I woke up from a coma with no memory of who I used to be. I am still the same person."

"I'm glad," Danny said. "I almost never use the pool. I work too much."

"That's just wrong," Allison said.

It was the end of August and strangely empty on the roof. There was one other woman at a round table beneath a beach umbrella, in shorts and a tank top, working on her computer. There was another woman in a lounge chair, reading an Emma Straub novel. And that was it.

"Ghost town," Allison said.

"Everyone works, I guess," Danny said. "There aren't a lot of kids in this building. Honestly, this is only my second time up here this whole summer."

"That's crazy," Allison said, but she was glad that it was empty. "I love it," she said. "I don't think I could have dreamed up this pool. Thank you for bringing me here."

"Of course," Danny said.

Allison swam laps, blissfully alone, in the pool.

Danny watched her swim.

After a while, Danny got in, too, and swam a couple of laps. Allison was faster than him.

"You're making an impressive recovery," he said. "This is pretty good after surgery."

"I was racing you," Allison said.

"That's not fair. I didn't know."

Allison agreed.

"Don't do too much, though," Danny said.

"Hey," Allison said. "Don't ruin my good time."

Allison was glad to be able to swim laps again. She took deep strokes. She felt weightless in the water. Her head did not hurt. She was still having headaches, but she did not tell this to Danny. When she felt done, Allison floated on her back, looking up at the sky.

"You can come swim here anytime," he said.

"I want to," Allison said. "I want to come every day."

"That's great," Danny said. "That makes me happy."

When Allison was done, Danny brought her back down to

his apartment to get changed for lunch. "Whatever you want to eat," he said. "We can order it."

That sounded good to her.

Danny told her she could get changed in his room.

Allison went to his room, closed the door. His bedspread was striped. Allison was glad.

The blinds were up and there was a view of New York. Allison felt exposed. She closed them. She sat down at the edge of the bed, contemplative.

Life had brought her here.

This was not the worst place.

In the end, she hadn't heeded Danny's advice about the laps. She had swum too much. Her head had started to hurt again, and she took a pain pill. She lay down on Danny's king-sized bed—just, she thought, for a second—and fell asleep, still wearing her bathing suit.

When she woke up, Danny was also lying on the bed, holding a book, but not actually reading it. Really, he was just looking at her, and he smiled at her, and Allison leaned over and kissed him. It was their second kiss, the first time since the kiss over Phoebe's head, and that was what Allison was thinking about when she pressed against him. When she slid the crotch of her bathing suit over to the side.

Phoebe.

She was thinking about beautiful Phoebe and how this was such a wonderful way to get a baby.

Allison had always loved pain pills, the way they made her feel. She used to take them sometimes just for fun, combining them with a glass of wine. She would sit on the deck of the movie producer's house and stare at the sky.

"We shouldn't do this, you know," Danny said, while in

the process of doing it. He held Allison's breasts, squeezing them on top of her bathing suit. Sliding his fingers beneath the elastic. "You're recovering. I'm your doctor. I don't want you to feel pressured."

Somehow Danny wanted Allison to stop him, but Allison was not going to do that. She had started it, and it felt good. It was what she wanted. She felt like she was back in the swimming pool, gliding through the water.

Danny had always been nice. Nice was not a quality that Allison had properly appreciated in her twenties. Allison was in her thirties now. Too many men had not been nice.

She had no interest in that. Never again. No more bad boys. Hipsters. Instead, she had found herself a rich doctor.

The idea of it made Allison smile. She had her hands on his back. She closed her eyes. Her old friend Danny. Allison had never had sex while still wearing a bathing suit. It created obstacles. She laughed. He laughed.

"Can we take this off?" Danny asked.

But Allison shook her head. She did not want to stop. That was always a risk.

And so they didn't.

Phoebe, Allison thought. *Phoebe.*

Swimming laps made Allison hungry.

Or maybe it was the sex.

Allison wasn't sure. But she knew that she was hungry and that she wanted something more than chocolate pudding.

This was exciting. It was the first time she had been hungry, really and truly hungry, since the cameraman smashed her on the head with a vase.

Allison remembered eating the croissant she had bought at the Starbucks on the turnpike. Taking off small pieces of the croissant, mushing them up in her hand, and then eating each bite as if she were a baby bird.

Danny had an impressive stack of menus.

New Jersey had changed since she was a kid. Danny had a menu for everything. Japanese, Korean, Italian, Mexican. Diner food. Ethiopian, even. Allison picked Indian. Samosas and saag paneer, and a chicken vindaloo, because Danny wanted something spicy, and an order of naan and raita. It all came in less than half an hour.

"This is amazing," Allison said.

Danny beamed, as if he had cooked the food for her himself.

He had a large selection of beers in his refrigerator.

"You are so hip," she told Danny, and he blushed.

He was not hip.

Allison would have run from him if he had been.

Allison picked an IPA from Brooklyn.

She felt happy. The Indian food and the beer. The swimming pool. Allison decided not to leave that night. Danny had an expensive coffeemaker and good coffee for the morning. She spent the next day in Danny's clothes. He would go to work and she would be alone.

"You'll be comfortable here?" he asked. "Do you need anything?"

Allison shook her head.

She sat on his sectional couch, drinking her coffee, looking out at the view. "I'll be fine," she said. "It's quiet. I like it here."

Danny said nothing. There was a look on his face that she did not understand. It might be love, but it seemed more like worry. Maybe it was worry that she was moving in. Allison did not think he could read her mind.

"Is it okay with you?" she asked him.

"It's okay with me," Danny said.

"Are you sure?" Allison asked, suddenly unsure.

"I'm sure," Danny said.

Allison was pleased. He was sure. He looked sure. They did not have to talk about what it meant if she stayed. Or what they would have for dinner that night when he got back.

"I'm going to swim laps," Allison said.

"That makes you happy," Danny said. "I like that. And then what?"

Allison shrugged. "I might take a nap. I might read a book or watch TV. I'll be fine."

"You won't get bored?"

"I won't," Allison said.

Danny leaned over and kissed Allison on the top of her head, troublingly near the hole in her head. Allison felt a shiver go down her spine.

In the end, though, Danny had asked her too many questions. She pretended not to be annoyed. Allison was glad when the door closed behind him and she could relax.

~~~~~~

Allison had noticed a hair salon in the lobby of Danny's building. She went down at ten o'clock when it opened. She wanted to get the haircut right away, before she lost her nerve. "I want you to shave it," Allison said.

The hairdresser had pink hair, which Allison had thought was a good sign. It reminded her of Missy, of course. Allison thought of Missy fondly, as if they had been good friends. The hairdresser—her name was Roxy—advised her not to shave her head.

"I wouldn't do that," she said. "It's going to look pretty short. Let's just give it a try and if you don't like it, I'll take it all off."

Allison decided to give it a try. The haircut was not perfect, but this was not the fault of the hairdresser. There was no way around the empty patch on her scalp, surrounding the hole in her head, but it was better than before. A cleaner look.

It was a new beginning.

"Your hair is going to grow back quickly," Roxy told her. "Besides that, this looks good. You have soulful eyes."

"I like you," Allison said.

Maybe that was a strange thing to say, but the hairdresser did not seem to mind.

"I like you, too," Roxy said.

"Maybe we can go swimming together," Allison said.

"That would be awesome," Roxy said. "I have always wanted to swim on the roof."

"You're not allowed?" Allison asked.

"Only tenants and guests."

"Can guests bring guests?" Allison asked.

"Maybe," Roxy said. "I would take the risk."

"Do you want to come today?" Allison asked.

"Oh," Roxy said. "I can't today."

Allison was surprised. Her feelings were hurt. Tears sprang into her eyes.

"Chlorine isn't good for dyed hair," Roxy said. "I just dyed it yesterday."

"I really like it," Allison said. "Your hair."

Her feelings were still hurt. It seemed unlikely that she would ever invite Roxy back to the pool again. It had been a bad idea, anyway. For now, she sat in the hairdresser's chair and gazed at herself in the mirror. This was a new Allison. An Allison with short hair.

Maybe her eyes were soulful, but she also looked a little bit sick. Allison wanted her hair back. But she did not want that large bald spot. She did not want another person to suggest that she cut her hair. Allison had seen the way her sister-in-law, and then her brother, had looked at her, then looked away, but somehow were still looking at her from the corners of their eyes, as if searching for the bald spot.

It was done. Allison gave Roxy a very large tip. She would not get her hair cut for a very long time, and so their friendship, as satisfying as it had been, was already over.

"Thank you, again," Allison said.

She listened to herself thanking the woman who had cut off all of her hair. It was not Roxy's fault.

This was better.

After the haircut, Allison went back to Danny's apartment.

The day was moving along.

She wanted to swim, but first she would call her mother. Her poor mother. She had left her a message on the answering machine the day before, but Allison knew that wasn't enough. Wasn't fair.

"I was so worried," her mother said.

"Now you don't have to worry," she said. "This is good for me. Really. Danny has a pool. It's what I need right now. To swim."

"You love to swim," her mother said.

Her mother still sounded worried. "Is there a lifeguard?" her mother asked. "On the roof?"

There wasn't a lifeguard at Danny's rooftop pool, but Allison told her mother there was one. Strategic lies were a good thing. A kindness.

Allison got into her bathing suit and took the elevator to the roof. She spread one of Danny's bath towels on one of the pool chairs. She spread suntan lotion on her arms, her legs, her face, her back, as much of it as she could reach without help from another person.

It was a sunny day. It was a hot day. It was a weekday. A Tuesday. Allison was the only person on the roof. She would be the only person in the pool.

Allison swam too much, because she could, until she was exhausted. She had trouble stopping, just because it was so nice.

Like the day before, it was incredibly quiet on the roof

of Danny's building. It was as if Allison was above the rest of the world. She was above the car horns and the beeping and the construction that somehow was everywhere. It was almost bliss, except for the fact that bliss had to be more than a rooftop pool in Fort Lee, New Jersey.

~~~~~

*T*hey quickly established a routine.

Danny left for the hospital early each morning, and Allison woke up alone in his fancy Fort Lee apartment. She made perfect coffee from a pod. She drank it sitting on Danny's sectional couch, looking out the wall of windows, onto the Hudson River.

"Hello, New York City," she said.

Until now, Allison had never been a fan.

She slept well because Danny Yang had a nice bed.

Danny was a brain surgeon and had an appreciation for the finer things and therefore possessed only quality things, which he was rarely home to use. He was gone all day, sometimes worked nights. He was, in many ways, the perfect boyfriend.

Allison was not entirely sure that he was her boyfriend. Since that very first morning, they had not discussed what it meant for Allison to be there. It seemed to be understood that she would stay.

Danny beamed when he came home each day, happy to see her.

Allison beamed back at him. After a day all alone it was nice to have the company. Allison rarely left the building, and when she did, she was careful not to walk by the hair salon.

Danny said that he liked her haircut, and that filled her with relief. Danny seemed to like everything about her. It was as if she were still his dream girl from college.

Her hair, she knew, did not look awful, but she did not like it short. It was also okay. Allison did not look in the mirror. It was better that way. Looking in the mirror somehow transported her back to the bathroom of the cameraman's house.

Looking in the mirror made Allison nauseated.

Her hair would grow.

After coffee, Allison went up to the roof and swam her laps in the swimming pool. She sat in the sun and wrote in her journal. Then she took the elevator back down to Danny's apartment. She ate breakfast. She took a pain pill and she slept through the afternoon. When she woke up, she watched TV. This all felt right to Allison. She was living the vacation life. Danny had an enormous flat-screen TV hanging on the wall of his living room.

One day, Allison received an email from her agent. Allison hesitated before reading it, but the news was good. Her script had gone into production. She would be receiving a check. Her agent wanted to know if Allison was working on something new.

"Not now. Just had brain surgery," Allison wrote back, which was, fortunately, an excuse for just about everything.

Her agent sent flowers to Allison's mother's house.

"They are beautiful," her mother called to say, and Allison promised to come pick them up. "Soon," Allison said. She did not believe herself.

The swimming pool on the roof would close soon and Allison did not want to miss a day. Danny would come home from work, around seven or eight, and they would order food. The food was always, always good. They had sex before falling asleep. Everything was fine. Allison did not know how Danny could bear it, going back into that hospital, day after day, but she did not ask.

On the weekends, other people would wander up to the swimming pool on the roof. Once or twice it even got crowded. That was not okay, but Allison started waking up early, and she was always able to swim her laps before too many idiots got into the pool. Danny swam with her.

"I wonder why I didn't do this before you were here?" he asked.

Allison did not know, either. She thought less of people who did not swim. Which was, honestly, most people. Most people, in Allison's opinion, were not particularly smart.

~~~~~

One day, after swimming laps, Allison found a voicemail on her phone from a police detective in North Carolina. They had found the cameraman. Would she please call? Allison had forgotten about the police, but they had not forgotten about her. It was unfortunate.

Still, she called back. There was something about a narrative arc. She couldn't not call them, as much as she didn't want to. She also wanted to know. Allison put a T-shirt on over her bathing suit, put her feet in the water, and, looking up at the sky, she returned the call.

The police in North Carolina had, really and truly, found the cameraman. Everything in Allison's story had checked out. The cameraman was, in fact, checked in to a psychiatric hospital. He was, in fact, bipolar. Everything he had written in the note turned out to be true. The detective wanted to discuss how Allison would like to proceed with the case. He wanted to know if she would like to press charges.

"We could get a conviction," the detective said. "He admitted to hitting you with the vase."

"He did?"

"He expressed regret."

"That's good," Allison said.

Somehow, she did not take any pleasure in knowing this. She looked up at the sky.

"We just need you to make a statement," the detective said.

"I already made a statement."

"You talked to police in New Jersey. We would need a new statement," the detective said. "You would have to press charges. The best thing would be for you to come to North Carolina."

"I don't want to go to North Carolina."

Allison actually needed to go to North Carolina.

She needed to figure out what to do with her house. It had blown down. The horrible neighbor had actually called, leaving a message on her cell phone. She did not remember ever giving him her number. Her horrible neighbor was upset about the state of things. He wanted her to clear away the debris. He wanted to buy her property. Allison did not want to sell it to him, because she did not like him. This sounded petty, but Allison had the right to be petty.

The detective on the phone mentioned her neighbor. Her neighbor had called the police. He had called the police on Allison. The city had removed the roof of her house from the street. The detective said that the city most likely had sent her a bill. Allison, of course, had not checked her mail in North Carolina. She had lived there for such a short time that she had not received a single piece of mail addressed to her. This was it, then. A bill from the city.

She no longer had a mailbox.

Allison, of course, did not want to do anything at all, but that did not seem to be entirely possible.

"I will think about it," Allison told the detective.

On TV, police detectives were often women. She did not understand why she couldn't get one of those. It would have helped. It was strange to have had this conversation sitting on Danny Yang's roof, her feet still in the pool. It was as if Allison had found a sanctuary and the police had decided to take that away, too. Allison ran her fingers through her hair, resting on the hole in her head. While her hair did not seem to be growing back as quickly as Roxy promised, it did feel incredibly soft. Allison ended the call. She promised to call back with a decision, but she knew that she would not call back.

North Carolina was over.

They could keep on sending her mail.

That part of her life was done.

It had not worked out for her. She was moving on. Like the movie producer had not worked out for her. Allison was fine. She was swimming laps. Allison looked at her beautiful swimming pool. She looked at her phone. She had an urge to throw it off the roof. It could kill someone. She would have to buy a new phone. Allison had a sudden urge to throw herself off the roof, but that did not make any sense.

Allison was fine.

Allison went back down to Danny's apartment and took a pain pill. She crawled into Danny's bed to watch TV and fell asleep. When she woke up, the TV was still on.

Allison touched her stomach.

Allison had forgotten about Phoebe.

"Fuck," she said out loud.

Allison did not know whether she was pregnant, but she was probably not supposed to be taking pain pills. Prescription narcotics. Allison knew she could look it up on the Internet. She could also ask Danny, but, like driving with a head injury, the answer was obvious.

"I'm sorry, Phoebe," she said. "If you are there. I will be better," she said. "I promise."

The baby, Allison thought, must be enjoying all of the laps. Swimming in Allison's belly while Allison swam in the pool. Phoebe would love to swim.

Allison was sure of it.

〰〰〰

The next day, after Danny left for work, Allison drank her coffee and she swam her laps. And then, before taking a nap and watching TV, she looked up the cameraman on her cell phone.

Keith #2. The police had told Allison his last name, but she had forgotten it. She had not written it down.

She put in his first name, the town in North Carolina, the name of the TV station. It was as easy as that. She could have done this long ago. She wondered what had taken the police so long.

Allison was able to find an address of the house, which apparently he owned, and then a picture of the house on Google Maps. Allison would have driven right by that house without any recognition. There were some marigolds planted in front.

Allison could see the driveway where her car had once been parked. She had been there, inside this house she'd found on the Internet.

Allison did not like to think about this part of her life. That made sense. Allison thought that the best way forward would be to try to forget about it. Allison stared at her cell phone, thinking that she would turn it off for the day, and then her cell phone rang, and Allison was so startled that she answered it.

It was her friend Lori, who, strangely, had not returned her call from the hospital.

"Where have you been?" Allison asked.

"Where have you been?" Lori asked.

"I had brain surgery," Allison said.

"Oh," said Lori. "Shit. I thought I heard that wrong on your message. Your voice sounded really weird. Loopy, like you were on drugs. I was worried that you were on drugs."

That, Allison thought, would have been a reason to call back.

"Maybe," Allison said, "that was because I had brain surgery."

"Oh shit," Lori repeated. "I'm sorry. I don't know why I didn't believe you."

"That's okay," Allison said, though it wasn't okay. She sighed. She kept the phone held up to her ear. She had talked last and so now it was Lori's turn.

"Are you okay?" Lori asked.

Allison considered the question.

"Sure," Allison said.

She had been okay, until the police from North Carolina called. Allison also wished that she had not googled the cameraman.

"So, my news," Lori said, "is that I am getting divorced. I gave up my apartment and I moved back home."

Allison could feel Lori's dramatic pause.

This was fine, actually. The timing was perfect. Allison did not want to talk about brain surgery, anyway. Allison knew you were not supposed to say "Yay!" when your friend told you she was getting divorced, though that was what she thought.

"Sorry," she said. "That sounds hard."

"Thanks, but actually, it *is* good," Lori said. "I needed to get out. It's better than having a husband. My mom babysits all the time and I am saving so much money on rent. Honestly, it had to be done."

"That's great then," Allison said. "Congratulations."

"Except for the fact that I am miserable."

"Well," Allison said.

"I know you never liked him."

That was not fair, of course, because Allison had never said this.

"I never said that," Allison said.

Allison knew that she hadn't. She had thought it but been careful not to say anything. She had not gone to the wedding. She was in Los Angeles at the time, so it was easy to say she couldn't make it.

"Where are you now?" Lori asked. "The hospital? Your mom's house? I could come see you. Honestly, I have nothing else to do today."

That, Allison thought, did not seem like a good reason to want to see her. Allison had been out of the hospital for two, maybe three, weeks. The days all blended together.

"Do you remember Danny Yang?" Allison asked.

"Of course," Lori said. "He had such a big crush on you. It was embarrassing to watch, how you used him for drives to the beach."

"I was not using him," Allison said. "We were friends. We went to the beach together."

"He had a really nice car," Lori said.

That was true. It was a BMW convertible. It used to belong to his father, before his father died. Allison had always liked going places in that car, the soft beige leather seats.

"Well," Allison said slowly, realizing she had not told any-one besides her mother where she was. Saying it out loud would make it real. But Allison liked it there. She had noth-ing to be ashamed of. "I am sort of staying with Danny. In Fort Lee."

"What?" Lori said. "Can you repeat that?"

"Fort Lee, New Jersey."

"Danny Yang?" Lori said. "You are staying with Danny. Are you with him? I didn't know you were still in touch."

"He was my brain surgeon."

"Your brain surgeon?"

Lori was a little bit slow in keeping up.

"He was."

"I love this," Lori said. "Danny Fucking Yang. Life is so fucking crazy sometimes."

Allison already regretted telling Lori. Maybe it was better not to have friends.

"Can I come over?" Lori asked. "I am going crazy here. I really want to see you."

The harm had already been done. Maybe it would be good to see a friend. To exist in the world, even though Allison regretted answering the phone.

The day was one big mistake.

She would get through it. Allison did not know how she could tell Lori not to come.

"What is the address?"

"I don't know," Allison said.

"You don't know?"

Allison didn't know. Danny had picked her up from her mother's house, and Allison had not felt it necessary to go out since then. When she wanted fresh air, she went up to the roof. There was a James Taylor song called "Up on the Roof" that she had listened to as a child. Allison was surprised that she hadn't thought of it until then.

"Are you a prisoner?" Lori asked. "Should I call the police?"

"No!" Allison said, much too quickly. "No police."

"It was a joke."

"No police," Allison repeated. She had started to shake.

"It was just a joke, Allison. I am not going to go to the police. But seriously. You don't know where you are? It's kind of weird that you don't know the address."

"It's one of those big high-rises," Allison said. "Near the George Washington Bridge."

It was sort of a monstrosity, really, the building.

"He lives there?" Lori said.

"That's where he lives."

"I know the buildings you are talking about."

"You do?"

"It's hard to miss," Lori said. "Which one are you in?"

"The one closer to the bridge."

"Okay, this is exciting. It's an adventure. I can find you. I'll tell you the address when I get there. How does that sound?"

"It sounds okay," Allison said. She did not say "great." She did not say "awesome." Allison was not sure how she felt about seeing Lori. "Bring your bathing suit."

"Hooray," Lori said. "I am so excited."

This was a good thing about Lori. She always wanted to swim.

*H*alf an hour later, Lori arrived with a bathing suit and a towel. "I wasn't sure which building it was, but I took a guess. I guessed right! I like your hair. I want to cut my hair. You look righteous. Seriously."

Allison had already swum her laps, so she just stood in the water, looking up at the sky, making a pattern with the palms of her hands. She went underwater and held her breath. She counted to ten and then came back up for air.

In contrast, Lori did a series of cannonballs into the water, making waves, creating new ripples on the surface of the pool. It had never occurred to Allison to jump into the pool. Allison was slightly dismayed by Lori's manic energy. But it was different, at least. Maybe the days had gotten a little bit boring, though that had not occurred to Allison until then.

"This place is insane," Lori said. "It's so over the top. So tacky. The lobby smelled like Febreze."

"Febreze?"

"This cheap cleaning product. You haven't noticed? It's disgusting."

Allison had not noticed. Maybe it was because she rarely stepped foot in the lobby, only went up to the roof.

"I'm hungry," Lori said after a while, and they went back to Danny's apartment. Allison handed Lori the stack of menus and Lori wanted Thai food. It was not part of her routine, but Allison decided that this was okay. The Thai restaurant had Danny's credit card already programmed. Allison had not expected to pay using his card, but it was easy, and Allison liked easy.

Life was strangely easy in Danny Yang's apartment. But for some reason, this lunch order made her feel guilty. She would tell him when he came home from work. She would pay him back. Maybe she would tell him about the email from the agent. The money coming her way. She could offer to contribute, to the rent, for the food, but that seemed awkward. And real, too real.

It would end soon, anyway.

The summer was coming to an end.

The rooftop pool would close.

Allison took out two beers from the refrigerator. She took a sip of her beer, and then she remembered Phoebe, and she did not drink the beer. Allison would be relieved when she got her period already and could drink again.

Allison blinked.

She wished that she had not thought that particular thought. It was as if she had jinxed herself. Allison and Danny had only had unprotected sex that one time. The odds were low, but Phoebe was still possible.

"My God," Lori said, walking around Danny's apartment, arms in constant movement. "This place is unreal. The view is GORGEOUS."

The view was, technically, gorgeous, but Allison had not fallen in love with it. She had not fallen in love with Danny's apartment. It was a bachelor pad. Everything was expensive and nice, maybe ordered from a store like West

Elm, definitely better than IKEA. Nothing, literally nothing, hung on the walls. There needed to be some rugs on the hardwood floors, but the floors were bare. They were nice hardwood floors.

Danny's dishes, the pots and pans they never used, were all of good quality. The appliances were expensive, shiny. The stove. The refrigerator. Dishwasher. Washer and dryer. It looked as if Danny had just moved in, but he had been there for two years. As he explained it, he worked a lot. A lot, a lot. Allison had begun to miss him during the day. It was nice, she realized, as Lori examined the apartment, waiting for the Thai food, to have the company.

"Danny Yang is doing well for himself," Lori said.

Allison agreed.

"I should have married a doctor," Lori said.

Allison agreed again.

They were both feminists who had careers in the arts. Marrying a doctor actually was a smart thing to do. This might not be a possibility for Lori, but it was something that she, Allison, could do. Marry a doctor. It was something she could consider, at least. She assumed that Danny loved her. It might also be kindness, convenience. When did Danny have the time to find a girlfriend?

Allison had no idea when her last period had been. Before the cameraman. Before the hurricane. She was not sure how long ago that had been. The buzzer to the apartment buzzed. It was loud. This was probably the one thing that was bad about this apartment. Usually Danny buzzed in the delivery person, opened the door for the food.

"You can let them in," Allison told Lori. Lori did not seem to find this strange.

The Thai food was good.

Pad Thai. A red curry. Tom kha gai soup. Allison felt grateful to live in a world where she could order Thai food and have it brought to her door.

She got out dishes, chopsticks, and they sat at the dining room table. Allison had never sat there before. She and Danny always ate in front of the TV. Allison felt disloyal for ordering food without Danny. She wished that he could be there, eating with them.

Did that mean she loved him?

Lori wanted another beer.

"Drink mine," Allison said. She did not want Lori drinking all of Danny's beer. "I'm not in the mood."

Lori talked about what it felt like to live in New Jersey again, about all the things in Brooklyn that she missed, but how, really, she didn't miss Brooklyn at all, because it was ridiculous, living packed so tightly into a small apartment, paying so much rent that she could barely afford to go out for coffee. She complained that all of these wonderful things about Brooklyn she could not take advantage of anyway, because she was always home alone with her daughter, Thea, and so what was the point?

Allison had met Thea when she was a baby. Thea was a toddler now. Lori complained about how hard it was to raise a baby without a partner, and Allison listened.

"You have to meet her," Lori said. Suddenly there were tears in her eyes. "She is the best thing in my life."

"That's great."

Lori showed Allison a picture of her daughter on her cell phone. She was a beautiful girl. Her hair was in two ponytails. She was wearing a red-and-white striped dress. "You are so lucky you had a girl," Allison said. "She's so beautiful."

"She is really beautiful, isn't she?"

"Oh my God," Allison said. "She is so beautiful."

"I'll bring Thea over next time," Lori said. "I would love to take her swimming."

Allison agreed. She was not sure Danny would want her to bring friends to his apartment, especially a friend with a small child, but she had to believe that he would. Allison listened to Lori talk and talk. She wondered if it mattered to Lori that she barely contributed to the conversation, but her friend did not seem to notice.

"I never thought this would be my life," Lori said, and then she started to cry.

Allison understood. She thought the very same thing, pretty much every day. It was not terrible, her life, it just wasn't what she had thought it would be.

"Your hair looks a little strange, honestly," Lori said. "I hope that doesn't hurt your feelings. It's a bold move, going that short. Why did you do that bald patch? It sort of looks like you have a hole in your head."

"I had brain surgery," Allison said. "I do have a hole in my head."

"Oh my God," Lori said. Clearly, she had forgotten about the brain surgery. "I didn't even ask you about that."

"That's okay," Allison said, staring at Lori's beer with longing. "I don't want to talk about it anyway."

~~~~~

Finally, Allison went to see her mother. It was the one-year anniversary of her father's death.

The dog barked. And barked.

"Hi, Gibson," Allison said. "Hi, Gibson. Good boy. You're a good dog. I love you, Gibson. Stop barking, Gibson. I'm here. I am petting you. Be quiet, Gibson. I love you, Gibson."

Allison sat on the steps and petted her mother's dog. He kept on jumping. Allison gently tried to push him back down.

"He's worried about you," her mother said. "He loves you."

Allison thought that this might be projection.

"I'm fine, Mom," Allison said. "I'm sorry if you were worried. It's easy for me to relax at Danny's place. It is a quiet place to recover. That's all."

Her mother had unpacked her suitcases and washed her clothes. Allison had ordered some clothes, a new bathing suit, but mainly she had been wearing Danny's things—boxer shorts and T-shirts, a blue sweatshirt—and somehow that felt all right. Danny had said something about Allison being in hiding, but that was not true. The outside world simply did not have an appeal.

Allison followed her mother to the dining room, where her clothes sat on the dining room table, perfectly folded, in neat piles.

"I threw out the things covered in blood," her mother said.

Allison's mother clearly wanted to talk about what had happened to her. Allison did not. Allison also did not want to talk about people that her mother knew, many of them strangers to Allison, who had cancer. Allison did not want to talk about politics, which, of course, was something many people talked about now. These, of course, were the main things that her mother liked to talk about. It was not fair that Allison was so closed down, that she made it so diffi-cult. Allison loved her mother. She had told herself, walking down the driveway after Danny dropped her off, that she would try.

"When is Adam coming?" Allison asked.

"He's not."

"Seriously?"

"Ava has a migraine," her mother said. "His wife. You know."

"I know who Ava is," Allison said, though she was also glad for the reminder.

"Your brother said he couldn't leave her alone with the baby."

This seemed like bullshit to Allison.

Also, Allison would have liked to see the baby. She would have liked to hold the baby in her arms. Kiss his hair.

Danny had offered to come, but Allison told him it was not necessary. He was also going to see his mother, and Allison said that two mothers in one day was a mother too many.

"I don't mind," Danny said. "Or I wouldn't have offered. But that's fine, if you don't want me to come."

Allison understood that somehow it wasn't fine. Clearly it was not fine. Allison understood that she was hurting Danny's feelings. He wanted to do something for her, and she did not want it. But he did not press her. There was sadness in his eyes as he drove away.

Of course there was no reason for him not to come, except that Allison did not want him to. She had not wanted to listen to her mother and Danny make conversation, but now she realized that would have been better. She could have listened to them talk. She would have been off the hook.

It also might have been nice, Allison realized, to have him there.

For her. He would have held her hand.

~~~~~

llison's mother wanted to take a walk at the Boat Basin.

"Your daddy loved it there," her mother said.

"That's a great idea, Mom," Allison said. "He did love it there."

It was a good idea. Allison was also glad to be leaving the house. Her mother started to cry. Allison hugged her mother and the dog started to bark. Gibson never liked to be left out.

"I miss Dad, too," Allison said.

"I know," her mother said.

"I hope you're not mad at me," Allison said.

"Why would I be mad at you?" her mother asked.

Allison shrugged.

Her mother put Gibson on a leash, put him into the back-seat of the car, and they headed out for the Boat Basin. They were, in fact, going back to Fort Lee, where Danny Yang lived. Allison's mother drove, taking a different route than usual, driving on the highway instead of the back roads. Right before their exit, Allison noticed Danny's building and its sister building taking up space in the sky. This, she understood, was why her mother had driven this way.

The buildings were tall and ugly.

It was better on the inside.

"That's where you live now?" her mother asked, pointing.

Allison got nervous when her mother took her hand off the wheel. She nodded.

"For now," Allison said.

It was not Allison's permanent residence. It was where she slept at night and where she woke up in the morning, where she swam laps. Where she ate her meals. Where she would return to with clean clothes later that night. But she did not live there. That was not Allison's life, was it? Danny's apartment in Fort Lee.

Danny Yang.

There was something tight in Allison's chest.

"Your father always wondered who would live in that building," she said. "Who would actually pay to live there."

"And now you know," Allison said.

"Is it nice?"

"The pool is nice," Allison said. She had told her mother about the swimming pool. Allison's mother understood how her daughter felt about swimming.

"That's good," her mother said.

"Lori said the lobby smelled like Febreze."

"Lori came over?"

Allison realized her mistake. She thought that her mother would like it, the fact that she had seen her childhood friend. But of course it was wrong to invite Lori to the apartment before her mother.

"Funny that it is you," her mother said. "Living there. Not just Danny. You. My precious daughter."

"Life is funny," Allison said.

"Life is funny," her mother agreed.

"Soon," Allison said. "You'll come over. It's just new. And I don't know how long I'll stay, so it feels weird to have guests."

"I don't see why that matters," her mother said. "I would have brought you your clothes."

Allison was used to living far away from home. Ever since graduating from college, she had lived far away.

"I don't want to overwhelm Danny," she told her mother.

Allison's mother exited the highway, the last exit before they ended up in New York City. Then they drove in the opposite direction from Danny's building, and then they were there, driving down the long, twisting road that led to the Hudson River.

It was a beautiful place. Allison's father had, in fact, loved it there. He used to take Gibson there on walks. Allison had been going to the Boat Basin for as long as she could remember. Her whole life. She had taken her father's picture with an actual camera, back in high school, walking the dog, a much larger dog, a standard poodle. She had printed that picture, in a darkroom, in black and white. He was wearing a striped polo shirt, smiling.

"I hate all of these people on their bikes," Allison's mother said, gesticulating with one hand, not passing the bicyclists until it was absolutely safe. She then cursed at a pack of joggers running in the middle of the road. "They are just out in the middle of the road, daring me to kill them. Are they insane? I think they are completely insane."

"It's okay, Mom," Allison said. "Just keep going slow."

Her mother was going slow.

Allison could see on the speedometer that her mother was

driving less than ten miles an hour. It was painful, not passing the bikers or the joggers; it seemed almost more dangerous, but they made it to the bottom.

Allison's mother parked the car in the parking lot and everything was okay again. Her mother scooped up dog from the backseat. Gibson licked her, wagging his tail.

"Hi, Allison," Allison said to herself.

Allison looked out at the Hudson River. It was the same view as from Danny's apartment, but also different. In the time that Allison had lived in Danny's apartment, it had never occurred to her to go there, to take an actual walk by the river. She had not gone for a walk, period; she had not explored the neighborhood. Sometimes, she took a walk around the perimeter of the rooftop. The edges were littered with cigarette butts.

"Your daddy would laugh at me," her mother said.

"Why would he do that?" Allison said. She could hear the suppressed irritation in her voice. "Why would he laugh at you?"

Allison did not want to talk about her father with her mother, but that was why they were out there. Allison still could not believe her brother was not with them. As if her brother thought that his life, his new family, was more important than they were.

"Because I miss your daddy so much," her mother said. "I had no idea I would miss him this way. Did you know that? He would laugh at me. Because he knew. He knew."

Allison, however, was not surprised. She knew her mother would miss him. They had been married for more than forty years.

Her father had wanted to spend winters in Florida. He

would have been happy with a week in Florida, but they did not go anywhere. Not even a day trip in the summer to the Jersey Shore. Once, they had come to visit Allison in Los Angeles, and her father had loved it. The palm trees. The sunshine. The Pacific Ocean. Her mother had loved it, too.

But that had been years and years ago. Now, her mother did not want to go anywhere. This trip to the Hudson River felt like an accomplishment.

Allison's mother took Allison's hand as they walked. It was nice to walk and not talk. The dog was being good, a normal dog, sniffing, peeing on trees. Not barking. Not jumping. The river was, in fact, really beautiful. Allison appreciated water in almost all forms, even if she could not swim in it. The act of looking at water was pleasing in itself.

Then Allison's mother started to talk again—it was inevitable—talking about everything that Allison did not want to talk about and things that she had not thought about, but especially did not want to talk about. Like the stack of mail that was waiting for Allison at the house. As the days went by and Allison did not return to retrieve it, Allison's mother had started opening, sure that she would save her daughter from some impending financial disaster. She had opened the bill from the hospital, for example, which was high, despite the fact that Allison had health insurance.

"I don't want to talk about this," Allison told her.

"You might not want to talk about it," her mother said, "but you have to pay the bill. Not talking about it won't make it go away."

"Mom," Allison said. "Please stop."

"You have to pay the bill or your credit rating will be ruined. You will be ruined."

"I'm not going to be ruined. I have money."

Allison remembered that she had a check coming, and she told her mother this.

Money mattered so much to other people. Allison could never understand rich people, for instance, always wanting more, working, running for political office, raking in astronomical, immoral salaries, instead of going to the beach, going for a swim. They could live on an island. Snorkel every day. Donate money to the needy. Eat well. That was what she would do. If she was rich.

Allison had not been able to grieve for her beach house, because the cameraman had smashed a vase over her head, and so she was grieving for herself instead. Allison wanted to grieve for her father, but her mother was making her talk about money, one of Allison's least favorite subjects. Maybe worse than a neighbor who had cancer.

"Let's sit," her mother said.

Allison just wanted to leave. Maybe she could walk back to Danny's. But they sat on a bench that overlooked the Hudson. Her mother put the dog on her lap and Gibson started licking her mother's face, licking her and licking her. The dog would not stop. Allison watched for what seemed like a very long time and then she looked away.

"Your daddy loved this dog," Allison's mother said. "He never cared that much about the other dogs, but this one he loved."

"I know," Allison said. "I know this."

Her mother had told her this, many times. It was not nice of Allison, however, to point it out. Allison wanted to be nice. Her mother did not seem to notice.

"This dog is such a comfort to me," her mother said.

"I know that," Allison said. "I'm glad."

It was terrifying to think that one day this dog would die, and then what would her mother do?

"I love you, Mom," Allison said.

~~~~~~

*I*t felt good to be back in Danny's apartment.

Allison felt grateful. She felt happy, even. She felt the urge to tell Danny that she loved him. "What do you want to order tonight?" he asked her.

"I don't know," Allison said.

She leaned over, kissed him.

"That's nice," Danny said.

There was something a little bit standoffish in his kiss. She really had hurt his feelings.

"Hey," she said, and she kissed him again, holding him tight so that he could not pull away. This time, he kissed her. "My mom was disappointed you didn't come," Allison said, not sure if this was actually true. "Next time, okay? I just wanted it to be family."

"How was the baby?" Danny asked. "Little Phoebe."

"My brother didn't come," Allison said.

They ordered Ethiopian.

It was hard to believe, but you could order Ethiopian food in Fort Lee, New Jersey. Growing up, Allison had had the choice of Chinese and pizza and McDonald's. McDonald's had been a big treat.

Allison loved Ethiopian food. The bread, especially: injera, soft, with the texture of pudding. Allison and Danny were both tired. They had both spent the day with their mothers. Allison had never felt comfortable in Danny's house in Tenafly. The living room was filled with antique furniture, all of it covered in plastic. The couch, the chairs, the white rug. "We only sit there on Christmas," Danny had explained.

Allison's head had begun to hurt, more than usual, and she had taken a pain pill. She had mainly stopped taking them. She liked them too much. She had not looked it up on the Internet, but she had a strong feeling that Phoebe would not like them.

Danny opened a beer. Allison shook her head.

"I'm not in the mood," she said, but she took a sip of Danny's beer.

She kissed him again, and then she lay her head against his shoulder.

"What?" Danny said. "Did you miss me?"

"I missed you," Allison said.

She worried that she had admitted too much. She did not want Danny to get attached to her. She did not want to become attached to him. She had heard of the rebound boyfriend. This, instead, was the brain-surgery boyfriend.

There was no way that it could be real. Their relationship. There was also the small chance that it could be fate. Or Allison was just getting in her laps while she could.

They kissed a little bit more, waiting for the food, but it didn't lead anywhere. Allison tried to unbuckle Danny's pants, but he stopped her. "The food is coming soon," he said.

"So we put our clothes back on," she said.

But the buzzer buzzed and Danny got up to get the food. Allison got a tray and brought the plates to the living room table. Danny's beer. Her seltzer. Napkins. Serving spoons. This was nice, their dinner routine, and Allison did not want it to end.

She also did not want the pool to close.

She had gotten another message on her voicemail that day from a district attorney's office in North Carolina, asking her to please return the call. Allison felt like there was a steady ticking in her brain. Reality was out there, waiting for her, and she wanted none of it.

She touched the hole in her head. It was still closed. The hair had begun to grow back in, a nice soft fuzz, like a baby's.

"I have a wedding to go to in a couple of weeks," Danny said.

"You do?"

"Do you want to come with me?"

Allison had started opening the plastic containers. She was impressed by the way the food had been packed. The injera was rolled the way you might find hand towels. It was clever. She unrolled the largest piece of injera onto her plate and began spooning the food onto the center. Greens. Spicy beef. It all looked so good.

She looked at Danny, waiting. She had learned as a child that it was rude to start eating before everyone else at the table. She hoped that Danny would stop talking soon.

"It's in Miami," Danny went on. "The wedding. It's a good friend of mine from medical school. The hotel is in South Beach. It's supposed to be a nice hotel. Right on the beach. A swimming pool. I can show you the website."

Allison looked at him.

It was as if he had said the magic words.

As if he knew that his pool would be closing soon and that

this wedding would ensure him more time with her. She did not know whether he knew what she was thinking. It made no sense, even to Allison, that she wanted to leave Danny Yang when the pool closed. She had only just realized that she loved him.

But maybe it was easy to mistake food and sex for love.

Or, maybe, that was what love was and she had the real thing.

"Sure," she said, nodding to herself. "I'll go. I would love to go."

Danny smiled, a surprised and relieved look on his face.

"That's great," he said. "I'll get you a plane ticket. My flight is already booked. Hopefully there is room on the same flight."

"Great," Allison said.

She thought about offering to pay for the plane ticket, but he had just offered to pay for it. Allison felt like the child in their relationship, more than happy to be taken care of. She wanted him to pay for everything. It was weird, really, considering that she had been raised a feminist.

"Can we eat?" she asked.

"Sure," Danny said. "Of course."

Allison tore off a piece of injera, took her first bite.

"This is so good," she said.

Danny grinned at Allison.

"The wedding will be fun," he said. Maybe he thought she would say no. "You'll meet a bunch of my friends."

They would go to a wedding together in Miami.

Life was already leading her to her next swimming pool.

~~~~~

Part
Five

*A*llison loved Miami Beach.

There were pelicans flying overhead, gliding over the water, and then torpedoing headfirst into the water. Pelicans! They looked like flying dinosaurs. They were glorious.

There had been no pelicans in North Carolina. There were no pelicans in Los Angeles. Or the Jersey Shore. The pelicans in Miami made Allison deliriously happy.

She floated on her back, up and down over gentle waves, and looked up at the sky. Out of the water, she took picture after picture of them on her cell phone.

"Pelicans!" Allison called out to Danny. "You didn't tell me there would be pelicans."

"I didn't know there would be," Danny said. "You like them so much!"

The surprising thing was that Danny did not seem to care about the pelicans beyond the fact that they pleased Allison. No one else on the beach clapped with delight when a pelican flew by. Allison could have looked at pelicans forever and ever. But Danny had told her that they would have to leave the beach soon. They were in Miami for a wedding, and apparently there were numerous wedding activities and duties required of him. More than just the wedding. At one point in the day, for instance, he had left her to join a volleyball game with his friends.

The worst part of this trip to Miami was the fact that they had to go to a wedding. Danny was part of the wedding party. One of several best men. They would not be there if it wasn't for the wedding, but that was beside the point.

After the beach, Allison and Danny stopped off at the hotel pool. It was a fine enough pool, but it was crowded with young and beautiful people. It was not a pool to swim laps in, but Allison did a couple anyway, just to feel her body move. She had to dodge hotel guests and could hear one of them curse her. Probably she had startled them, but Allison was also cursing the people in the pool, blocking her way. Allison was surprised by the anger she felt. She did like the cool, clean, chlorinated water after the ocean, and it was an expensive hotel, but Allison did not like this pool, the scene. Everywhere there was music playing. Even underwater, through underwater speakers, there was music playing. Allison loved the quiet of swimming. The music was all wrong.

Danny ordered their drinks, and he brought them to a table. A gin and tonic was waiting for her when she got out. It was what her father would drink if he had ever gotten the chance to stay at an expensive hotel in Miami. The trip she was taking was an unattainable dream for him.

She would not drink her drink, of course. But she would take a sip. She had ordered the G&T for her father. She had ordered the drink so that Danny would not suspect a possible Phoebe.

Phoebe was Allison's secret.

"You look melancholy," Danny said, and Allison shook her head.

"No," she said. "I'm not."

"You're not?" Danny said.

"I'm not."

Danny drank his beer.

Allison took a sip of her drink. It was delicious.

"Hi, Dad," she said. "This one's for you."

Her father wasn't there with her. He wasn't a presence at the pool or the beach. He hadn't been at the hospital when she was there, either.

Allison's father was in an urn in a box somewhere in her mother's house. Allison did not feel his spirit. He was not a lingering ghost, although Allison would have liked that.

~~~~~

Danny had told Allison about the rehearsal dinner, but she had not realized that he expected her to go with him.

Allison had packed only one nice dress for the wedding. She actually did not like this nice dress. She had bought this dress to wear to a film premiere in Los Angeles for one of the movie producer's movies. The dress was short, form-fitting. Sexy. Allison looked good in it, but she also hated wearing it. She had bought the stiletto heels, too, which she had worn only that one time. She'd packed these for the wedding, too.

Allison had not enjoyed the film premiere, the kind of event that she normally loved, because she was so uncomfortable in her clothes. All night long, men had stared at her cleavage.

Somehow, it was the only dress Allison owned.

While packing her suitcase for Miami, Allison remembered how much she had hated wearing this dress. She did not, however, have any other suitable dresses or time to order another one. Allison had nothing appropriate to wear to a rehearsal dinner. She told Danny this at the hotel pool bar. She took a second sip of her drink. So good.

"It's okay," Allison said, putting it back down. "I won't go."

I don't really know any of your friends. You'll have a better time without me."

Danny did not seem pleased with this answer. He had not told her, when he invited her to this wedding, that she would have responsibilities.

"Are you sure?" Danny said. "I would like you to come. There's a boutique in the lobby of the hotel. Do you think you could find something there?"

"Boutique" was a strange word to hear from his lips, but that was what it said on the glass window of the clothing store in the lobby of the hotel. It was annoying. The necessity of two events. Two outfits. It was only a three-day trip.

Allison also was his date. He had paid for her plane ticket, which felt appropriate, but it also then felt fair that she play the role of wedding date. Allison was not against marriage, but she hated weddings. She wondered why she had not thought of this right away when Danny had invited her to come.

"I can look," Allison said.

"That would be great," Danny said.

So Danny went back up to the room to shower and Allison went to the boutique. She could do this, of course. It was almost easier because she had only one store in which to find a dress and only ten minutes in which to do it.

There was even a dress that she liked: a sleeveless, loose-fitting, gray silk dress that went down to her ankles. She loved it, actually. The movie producer would have hated it.

She felt lucky to have found a dress that she loved. It almost felt like a miracle. She took it up to the cash register and handed over her credit card. There she was, paying for something herself like an actual person in the world, which she actually was. Maybe Allison had forgotten that, having spent weeks alone, up on a roof.

There was a vase of flowers on the counter of the boutique. Waiting to pay, Allison had a sudden urge to smash this vase on someone's head. Anyone. Another customer. The pretty woman in a sequined dress refolding T-shirts.

There were only women in the store.

None of these women deserved this kind of violence.

The urge passed as quickly as it came.

Allison dropped her wallet on the floor. She bent down to pick it up. She felt dizzy.

"Are you okay?" the salesgirl asked her. She was the one in the sequined dress. She stopped folding T-shirts to let Allison pay for her purchase.

Allison had the urge to touch one of the sequins.

Allison felt like her brain was possibly wired wrong.

That would be Danny's fault.

Allison said that she was.

She was okay.

I have my health, she thought, and she smiled, amused by the running joke still playing in her brain. She did not think anyone else would think it was funny.

Allison was signing the receipt for her dress on an iPad screen when her cell phone rang. Allison was not going to answer, but her phone rang so rarely that she decided to look.

It was her brother.

Her brother never called her. They communicated only through email and text. This made Allison think that something must be wrong. With her mother. With the baby. With her mother's dog. With his wife, who was prone to migraines.

"Hey, little sister," Adam said.

"Adam?" Allison said. "What's going on? Is something wrong with Mom?"

Allison accepted her purchase from the smiling sequined salesgirl. Her lipstick, Allison realized, matched the sequins. This was clever, Allison thought. Attention to detail. Allison's dress was wrapped in tissue paper and put into a shiny paper bag with string handles. It was such a waste, all this packaging. But Allison felt that it would be odd to put the dress into her purse, which was probably filled with sand.

"Wrong? No," Adam said. "Nothing's wrong. I am going to bring the baby for a visit with Mom tomorrow if you want to come to the house."

"How is Phoebe?" Allison said without thinking.

"Who is Phoebe?" Adam said.

Allison realized her mistake.

She wondered how she could play it off and realized that she couldn't. She thought she could ask about her brother's wife, but at that moment, she had forgotten the name of her sister-in-law, too. Allison looked at the vase on the counter. It was filled with water. Flowers. It would be very different from her own experience to attack a person with this vase. She would probably want to take out the flowers first, pour out the water.

Allison zipped her purse shut so that she would not lose her wallet. Allison had lost her wallet before. It happened when she was distracted.

"The baby," Allison said. "How is the baby?"

She still did not know his name.

She did not think it would come to her.

"You mean Keegan," Adam said. "My son? That Phoebe?"

"Hey, Adam," Allison said. "This is actually a bad time to talk. I don't think you know this, but I'm in Florida," she said. "It's a bad connection. I will call you back later."

It actually was hard to hear him. There was music in the boutique, of course, like everywhere else in the hotel. Allison took her beautiful gray dress, now in the shopping bag that she would soon throw away in her hotel room, and she walked into the lobby, where there was the same music playing even louder.

Allison had thought she liked Miami, and probably she did. The pelicans. She loved the pelicans. Maybe it was only the expensive hotel she did not like. Allison had to concentrate in order to locate the elevator.

Her brother, Allison realized, was still on the phone. He had not said goodbye the way he was supposed to.

Allison found the elevators. There was a large group of people, waiting. Allison had a deep, ingrained hatred of crowded elevators. This had not been a problem in Danny's building, since she almost always went up to the roof. Allison wished that she had not told Danny to go to the room without her. She had not wanted him in the boutique, but she did want him now, to hold her hand. She wondered if she could call him now, ask him to come down, so that they could ride back up together. She would not do that, tempting as it was.

"What are you doing in Florida?" Adam asked.

"I'm with Danny," Allison said. "We're going to a wedding. One of Danny's friends from medical school. I just bought a dress to wear to the rehearsal dinner."

"Then you can't see Keegan tomorrow?" Adam said.

Keegan. It was such a strange name. Allison wondered why

her brother had agreed to a name like that. It did not sound like something he would name a baby. Probably it was a popular name.

"Allison?" her brother asked. "Tomorrow? Will you be back?"

"Um, Adam," Allison said. "There's no way I could be back by tomorrow. I am in Florida. We fly back on Sunday."

Allison could hear the silence on the other end of the phone. This was not her fault. It was not as if she did not want to see her beautiful nephew, even though he was not a girl. She understood that her brother was angry at her, and this made everything harder. Why was he angry? Why would she want to spend time with someone who was angry with her? He could try to be nice. He had not come for the anniversary of her father's death. He could have come. Or maybe Ava really was sick. But it seemed like he should have come.

"I am really sorry, Adam. I would love to see your baby."

Watching the lights of the elevator, following the progress of the elevator as it came down, Allison forgot the name of her nephew again.

"I totally fell in love with him," she said. "At first sight." This was true, had not changed. Maybe he would like to hear that. "It's just that I went away for the weekend and so it's impossible for me to see him or I would. I mean, I know it does not seem that way, but I do have a life."

Almost a month had gone by. Allison had lived in Fort Lee all that time. She had not made an effort to see the baby since her first day out of the hospital. The blame, of course, fell on her. Her priority had been to swim every day until the pool closed.

When Allison returned to New Jersey, the pool would be closed. And she would see her nephew then.

An elevator came to a stop and an impossibly large group of people emerged, one after another, as if from a clown van, women in heels, men in button-down shirts, all of them talking, talking, every single person, collectively, much too loud, and Allison was afraid that these were people who would be at the rehearsal dinner.

Allison was about to step into the empty elevator when the crowd that had amassed around her piled in first. She did not move to get on it. She watched it go. She would wait for the next one. There would be another elevator, like in New York City, where, if you had faith, there would be another subway, hopefully not as crowded.

"So, you're living with your brain surgeon?" Adam said. Allison was holding the phone to her ear, but, monitoring the elevator situation, she had forgotten about her brother. She was running out of time. She had to get ready for the dinner. "I didn't believe Mom when she told me," Adam said.

Allison did not understand why her mother had to tell Adam anything at all. Her life was her business. Also, she was not living with Danny. She had floated there, a soft landing with a swimming pool in order to recover from trauma. That had been Lori's word, *trauma*, during the few minutes they had talked about Allison. Allison wanted to skip this rehearsal dinner, but she had bought a dress. She liked the dress, wanted to wear this dress. She did not want to disappoint Danny. She did not understand why she was denying her relationship with Danny.

Danny was great.

"I have known Danny for years," Allison said to Adam,

wondering why she was justifying herself. The next elevator was coming down again. "Since college."

"I just got off the phone with Mom," Adam said. "She didn't tell me you were away."

It was as if her brother had caught her in a lie and was pleased with himself for pointing it out. As if, because he had talked to her mother, that meant that Allison wasn't in Florida at all, and could still come to see the baby.

"It was very last minute," Allison said. "I just bought a dress," she said. "For the rehearsal dinner. Which is in half an hour so I have to go."

The last rehearsal dinner, Allison realized, that she had been to was her brother's. His wedding, too. Many months later, her brother had told her that she had not behaved well. She had not, for instance, gone to the bridal shower. She had not danced at the wedding. She had not made a toast. She had not stayed until the end. Allison, however, had not realized that any of these things were required of her. She thought it was enough to attend. To pose for family pictures.

"Adam," she said. "I really have this rehearsal dinner to get ready for. I'm waiting for the elevator. I can't concentrate. It's really loud in the lobby. I have to get on the elevator. I can't talk right now."

"You know you have only met Keegan once," he said.

"OMG," Allison said, surprising herself. When had she ever said OMG before?

"He's just a baby. It's not too late. I will see him next weekend," Allison said. She could not keep the exasperation out of her voice. "I totally promise you."

"Next weekend could work," Adam said. "But only if you can come out to me."

"Okay," Allison said. "Sure. Fine. I can do that."

There was silence on the other end of the phone. It was almost hard to hear it in the noisy hotel.

"I had brain surgery, you know," Allison said.

"You said you were fine."

"I am fine."

Allison wondered how much longer she would be able to use brain surgery as an excuse.

All of her life, she decided. That was how long it should work for her. Her brother was already impatient with her. The rest of the world did not care.

"We're busy on Saturday," Adam said.

"So Sunday then," Allison said. "I'll drive."

It was time for her to start driving again. She had a car, though the battery was probably dead. She would have to get it jumped. Real life sometimes felt much too hard. "Maybe I'll bring Mom. I have to go now."

"You're not getting married, are you?" Adam joked. "Eloping with your brain surgeon?"

Allison shook her head.

Another elevator opened again, and again she did not get on it, but that was fine. She would not be the kind of person who talked on her cell phone in a crowded elevator.

"God no," she said.

"Good," he said, laughing.

It was a relief, to hear the anger gone from his voice.

Allison loved her brother.

When she was little, she even had a big crush on him, as if he was a movie star. Allison was about to tell Adam how much she looked forward to seeing him next week, but he spoke first.

"You are much too selfish to get married," he said.

"What?"

Allison closed her eyes.

She felt a sudden burst of fury, as if there was actual fire in her brain, the hole in her head pulsing red. She touched it, almost expecting it to open and erupt, hot lava flowing from the source, burning the hotel down to the ground.

~~~~~

An elevator door opened, and this time Allison stepped in. This elevator was empty, and Allison felt profound relief. She deserved this empty elevator. She pressed the close-door button, watching as the door shut in front of a group of teenagers in bikinis running to catch it. One girl stuck her arm in and the closed door opened again.

"Didn't you see us?" the girl said.

Allison said nothing.

It was good that for the most part weapons were hard to obtain. Allison did not believe that these girls deserved to live. Didn't they understand that this elevator belonged to her?

Of course, there was music playing in the elevator. The same music that had been playing in the lobby. It was loud, again, too loud for such a small space, and the teenage girls were also loud. Everything did not need to be this hard.

Allison crossed her arms over her chest. She took a deep breath. Told herself she was fine. She was fine. This was not like escaping a house where a cameraman might emerge from any possible direction with a flowerpot or a hunting knife. A machine gun. This was not a horror movie. This was a fancy hotel. An elevator. But what if the elevator stopped and she was stuck in it with the teenage girls?

The elevator dinged, the door opened, and even though it was not her floor, Allison rushed out. Her heart was pounding.

Allison found the stairs at the end of the hall and ran up three flights and then ran down the hall, looking for her room. Standing in front of the door, she realized she could not find her key card. She checked her pockets. She checked her wallet.

She knocked on the door.

She knocked hard.

She was impatient. Angry. Angry at her brother, angry at the girls in the elevator, angry at Danny for not opening the door right away.

"What happened?" Danny said. "What happened? Are you okay? Allison?"

"What?" Allison said. "I'm okay. I'm fine. The elevator was crowded. I lost my room key."

Danny looked worried, and not in a normal way. He looked worried like he might hold a light up to her eyes and ask her to follow his finger.

"I got a dress," she said. "Are you happy? It's really nice, actually. The elevator was crowded. Three elevators in a row and all of them were full. I took the stairs."

Allison needed to regain control of herself. She did not want to talk to Danny this way.

She did not want to talk to Danny at all. It would be better for both of them if she didn't.

"I need to take a shower. Is that okay with you? Do I have time for a shower?"

"Yeah," he said. "Sure. Not a lot. But, of course. Are you feeling all right?"

"If you ask me to follow your finger with my eyes, I swear I am going to hit you."

"Allison?" Danny said.

Allison did not bother to explain. Apologize. She went into the bathroom and locked the bathroom door. She looked at herself in the mirror. There she was. Her hair still short. Roxy had lied. Maybe it would never grow back and she would always look like this. She also looked like she had gotten a little bit sunburned. Allison closed her eyes and when she opened them, she saw the other Allison, blood-shot eyes, green skin. Blood in her long, matted hair. Vomit on her chin. For a moment, Allison thought she would throw up.

"Don't," she said to herself. "Don't."

Allison did not want to vomit. She was fine. She was fine. She felt the vomit begin to rise and then go back down. She was not going to throw up, even though she tasted it in her mouth.

"You're fine," she said to the woman in the mirror.

Allison turned on the shower, running the water hot. It was a good hotel shower. There were expensive bath products in this bathroom. There was no music playing in this bathroom. It was blissfully quiet.

Allison sat down on the floor of the shower. She touched the hole in her head. It would be funny if it was an actual portal. What would it do? Shoot out fire? Provide turkey sandwiches when she was hungry? She tried to remember what had happened in the story about the guy with a hole in his head. It was probably the worst story she had ever read, but that was all she remembered.

Allison desperately did not want to go to this rehearsal

dinner. She would not go. She could do that. She would say she had a headache. An awful headache. She felt pleased with herself. It was a perfect lie. What could Danny, her brain surgeon, say? What could he fucking say to her? Would he force her to go? He would tell her to rest. That was what he would do.

And she was right.

He told her to rest.

Just like she knew he would.

〰〰〰

Allison hated weddings.

Or maybe, more accurately, she hated wedding receptions. All the money poured into a party. She would find herself becoming self-righteous. She would inevitably start thinking about all of the suffering in the world while standing at the open bar. All of the artists' grants one reception could fund. Allison did not like to dance to cheesy music in a hotel ballroom. Sit at some round table, eating salmon, forced to make conversation.

Because of a baby that was not even a baby, Allison wouldn't even be able to drink. The only redeemable part of a wedding reception. Allison looked at the piece of salmon on her plate. If she ate the salmon, she would have something to do.

Getting dressed, Allison had realized that she did not have to wear the movie premiere dress. Not for the wedding. Not ever. She threw the movie premiere dress in the trash. She threw away the high-heeled shoes.

Instead, she wore the gray silk dress from the boutique that was supposed to have been for the rehearsal dinner. She wore her sandals. She attended the ceremony with her short hair still wet, because she could not bear the sound of the hair dryer. It did not matter anyway, because she barely had any hair.

"I like your dress," Danny said.

"Thank you," Allison said.

He did not say a word about her sandals. About her wet hair. Danny Yang appeared to be slightly afraid of her, scared of saying the wrong thing, something that, in fact, he could easily do.

Danny appeared glad, grateful even, that she had agreed to come to the wedding at all. Allison was sad that it had come to that. But, also, she did not feel like not being scary. Allison felt tricked. Somehow, she was in a relationship. Danny had saved her life and therefore she was supposed to love him, be in love. And she did love him. All of this had somehow led to being at a wedding in Miami. Showing up as Danny's date, Allison realized, was considered significant. She had liked their relationship better without a label.

During the reception, Allison sat at her appointed spot at the round table, growing more and more angry. She did not eat the salmon. And, at some point, near the end of the night, she surprised herself by getting into an argument with a bridesmaid about karma.

The bridesmaid had also been seated at Allison's table and she had taken off her stilettos. All of the bridesmaids were wearing stilettos. Danny was out on the dance floor, even though Allison was unwilling to dance. He appeared to be having a good time.

Allison did not mean to get into an argument with the bridesmaid. It felt like she was being baited. It felt like she had no choice.

The bridesmaid was drunk.

The bridesmaid said something idiotic about how the

bride must have been good in her previous life. How the bride had this amazing karma. How karma had to be the only explanation for how lucky the bride was. According to the drunk bridesmaid, the bride had the perfect husband, the perfect wedding, the perfect life. The poor bridesmaid wanted all of this for herself.

A spaghetti strap kept falling off her lavender-colored dress, and she kept on pulling it up. Allison hoped that this bridesmaid would not have sex with anyone that night. This was what people did at weddings. A long time ago, Allison had had drunken sex after a wedding.

"I don't believe in karma," Allison told the drunken bridesmaid.

"What? What do you mean?" The bridesmaid rubbed her eyes. "How can you not believe in karma?"

"I have thought about this before," Allison said. She had. "Karma," Allison said. "Reincarnation. That whole idea of getting the life that you deserve. It's bullshit."

"What?"

"It's bullshit," Allison said, repeating herself. She realized that she might seem drunk, but she was, of course, completely sober. "Seriously," Allison said. "Explain the Holocaust to me."

"The Holocaust?" The bridesmaid looked alarmed at being made to even think about the Holocaust at a wedding. "What are you talking about?"

"Yes. Exactly," Allison said, knowing that she should stop herself. "The Holocaust," Allison said. "Six million Jews killed in concentration camps. Not to mention all the gays and the gypsies. There was nothing," Allison said, "not a single fucking thing these people could have ever done in a previous life to deserve that kind of karma. Getting gassed in an oven."

The bridesmaid looked stunned.

Allison would not be surprised if this bridesmaid started to cry.

"You don't agree?" Allison did not wait for the bridesmaid to answer. She knew that she was right.

There was no such thing as karma. Luck, maybe.

Good luck.

Bad luck.

Global warming.

Allison would do anything for a drink. She had gotten through the entire wedding reception completely sober, making this enormous sacrifice for a baby that probably wasn't there. It was only that one time they'd had unprotected sex. Allison could look it up on Google. Probably you couldn't get pregnant right after having brain surgery.

Anyway, she should get some good karma for this. Proving to Phoebe, at least, that she was fit to be a mother, by not drinking. As if Phoebe was testing her, already. But Allison did not believe in karma. Allison felt overwhelmingly sad, suddenly, that Phoebe would probably never get to see a koala bear. It was horribly selfish for Allison to even want a Phoebe.

"You're not convinced?" she asked the bridesmaid. "I could go on," Allison said. "If you aren't convinced."

"What?" The bridesmaid actually gasped and Allison realized that she was enjoying this, tormenting a stranger in a lavender dress.

This was why Allison did not usually engage in conversation with strangers. Because she got into trouble. Allison knew she was right. About karma. About, basically, all of her deep-held beliefs. It did not matter what other people thought. Allison also knew that there was nothing she could say that would change this bridesmaid's mind.

The bridesmaid did not respond.

"Okay," Allison said. "Let's talk about animal extinction. Think about the animals. The koala bears. Do you know how many are left on the planet? After the bush fires in Australia," Allison said. "Not a lot. How many different species are going extinct, right now, because of climate change? Is that karma?" Allison asked. "Do these poor, innocent creatures deserve to die? All the fish reliant on the coral reefs? Baby turtles. Do they have bad karma?"

Allison actually did not know the statistics about baby turtles. Maybe they were fine, but probably they weren't. She leaned across the table and pulled up the strap of the bridesmaid's dress, which had fallen back down. This bridesmaid was so vulnerable. It was almost heartbreaking. It was lucky for the bridesmaid that the reception was in the hotel and that she would not have to figure out how to get home. Unless she got picked up in the elevator by some asshole. It could happen. She could be raped in her own hotel room tonight. This would not surprise Allison, but she did not see how she could protect her.

The drunk bridesmaid started to cry.

Bingo.

It was unfortunate but inevitable.

"I'm sorry," Allison said. And she was.

This was not who Allison wanted to be. She wanted to protect this bridesmaid from elevator date-rapists. Instead, she was causing her pain.

Allison was like an abused person inflicting abuse on others.

This thought stunned Allison.

She had never before thought of herself this way.

She wanted to stroke the bridesmaid's hair, but, instead, she watched her cry.

〰〰〰

The bride herself came over.

Allison hadn't seen her approach. The bride had been wearing a ridiculous wedding gown but had changed into something simpler after the wedding. A short white dress with spaghetti straps, like her bridesmaids.

The bride kneeled behind the bridesmaid's chair and hugged her from behind. "It's okay, Tracey," the bride said, kissing the top of her friend's head. "It's okay."

Allison reached for the hole in her head. Still closed. Hair was actually beginning to grow over the wound. A soft fuzz. Like a baby duck's.

Tracey. The bridesmaid's name was Tracey. It was a ridiculous name. A name suitable only for a bridesmaid.

Allison did not know the bride, but she knew that she was a doctor. The bride and the groom had both gone to medical school with Danny. So why the hell had she dressed her friends in those godawful lavender dresses? Was that kind? Tears were streaming down Tracey's face. She had long streams of black mascara oozing down her white cheeks.

Danny, Allison realized, was probably the only minority at the wedding, though really Danny wasn't a *minority* minority. All of his friends were white. He barely spoke any Chinese. He spoke to his mother in English. But that didn't make him not a minority, either. It only meant that he was, basically, invisible. Not seen by his friends, not even by Allison. She was no better than anybody. She just wanted to go back underwater, the pool or the ocean. She was done with this wedding.

The bride kept stroking Tracey's hair.

Allison had really not said anything that awful. She thought that the Holocaust and global warming were in the back of everybody's minds. Or should be. A frame of reference.

"It's okay, sweetheart," the bride said. "You don't have to cry. Tonight is a happy night."

"I know," the bridesmaid wailed. "I know it is."

The bride turned to look at Allison. To glare at her, really.

"I'm sorry," Tracey gushed. "I am so happy for you. This wedding is so beautiful."

"It's really nice," Allison said. She could see Danny from the corner of her eye. The bride had come over to monitor the situation. Why hadn't he?

Danny was on the other side of the room now, drinking a beer, talking with his guy friends. They looked ridiculous in their tuxedos. He had taken off his bow tie. He should really be here, comforting her, the way the bride was comforting Tracey.

"This is a great party," Allison said, thinking this was a safe thing to say.

"I don't think we know each other," the bride said. She smiled at Allison.

The bride was one of those people who could manage to be pleasant even when pissed off. That was a skill Allison had never acquired. She did not have much use for phony people.

"I'm here with Danny," Allison said.

The bride's face was blank.

"Danny Yang," Allison said. "Best man. Brain surgeon. You went to medical school with him."

All of Danny's friends knew him as Daniel. Allison remembered this now. Allison did not know this Daniel. She was not sure if she liked him.

Daniel Yang was the kind of man who, for instance, played group volleyball. Allison would never go out with a man like that.

"Oh," the bride said. "Daniel. Of course. He didn't RSVP for a plus-one and then, at the last minute, he texted he was bringing someone, and we had to readjust all of the tables."

"How awful for you," Allison said.

She, of course, was the plus-one.

"I'm glad he brought a date," the bride said. "It was just so much work to figure out at the last minute."

"That's me," Allison said.

"Oh," the bride said. She smiled at Allison.

Probably the bride did not think she was good enough for Danny. With her weird short hair and her long, comfortable dress.

"We were talking about karma," Tracey said.

The bride put a napkin in a waterglass and was cleaning Tracey's face.

"I think we should only talk about happy things at a wedding," the bride said, and Allison nodded.

"Only, somehow," Allison said, "I never stop thinking about horrible things."

The bride did not look surprised by this admission.

"This is my happy day." The bride looked at Allison, and

Allison realized she was being delivered a command. "Do you think you could try?"

"She is so awful," Tracey murmured, as if, somehow, Allison could not hear this. As if her feelings would not be hurt. The bride continued to clean Tracey's face. Allison thought she should move. She could go to the bar and get a nonalcoholic beverage. She could get a piece of wedding cake.

But Allison stayed in her seat. Her head had started to hurt. Allison did not think that that was because of brain surgery. She thought it was the loud wedding reception music. Because of the confrontation. The confrontation was Allison's fault, but it still upset her. It was not fair.

It wasn't fair.

Finally, Danny came over. He sat down in the empty chair next to hers. He put his arm around her. Allison leaned into him. Suddenly, she wanted to cry. It was not just the bridesmaid having a hard time. Allison realized that she was crying. But maybe it was hard to tell, because she wasn't wearing mascara. Allison wondered why he had let her get into this mess in the first place. He was her brain surgeon. Wasn't he supposed to protect her?

"I am so glad you are meeting everyone," he said to Allison. It was a polite thing to say, but Danny was not stupid. He could see the look on her face. He was there—at last—to rescue her. Allison was angry at him, but also glad.

"Congratulations, again," he said to the bride. "This has all been so great. The wedding. This whole weekend. I am so happy for you and Kyle. I always knew you two would tie the knot."

The bride smiled at Danny. She had a confused look on her face, too. Allison wondered if Danny had brought inappropriate girlfriends to other parties in the past. It did not seem like something he would do.

"Allison and I went to college together," Danny said to the bride. "We have been having such a great time in Miami. Allison loves the pelicans."

Danny kissed the top of her head.

If he told the bride about her brain surgery, she would kill him.

"I'm so glad," the bride said.

"It looks like Tracey had a little too much to drink," Danny said. He was winning points back, at least, defending Allison.

Allison could not blame him for his friends, but then, she also could. Why was he friends with these people?

"Can we leave?" Allison whispered into his ear.

"Yes, we can leave," Danny whispered back, squeezing her hand. He was smart not to reprimand her. "I'm sorry I left you alone. I know this is not your kind of thing. I wasn't thinking."

Danny held her hand and they started walking. They had made it out of the ballroom when Allison could hear the booming voice of the DJ, making some kind of announcement, and a cheer came from the wedding party. Allison had not ruined this wedding. The bridesmaid had already been drunk; she was already unhappy. Clearly, it was the bridesmaid, Tracey, who had bad karma.

Only, Allison did not believe in karma.

Allison did not deserve what had happened to her.

The cameraman. The vase smashed over her head.

Allison wanted her ramshackle beach house back. She wanted her life back. The cameraman had tried to take it from her. He had stolen it from her. She had not realized it until that moment. The cameraman had taken something from her, but she didn't know what it was.

There was a hole in her head.

It did not feel closed.

She was not ready to move on.

Allison shut her eyes and there they were: the orange and white cats. The cameraman did not deserve to have them.

〰〰〰

They took off their wedding clothes.

Allison watched as Danny left his tuxedo crumpled on the floor. She turned on the TV. She flipped through the stations.

Danny lay on the bed next to her, eyes closed. He had drunk too much, which was another thing people did at weddings. Allison would have done it, too, but now she was glad that she wasn't drunk. Would not be hungover in the morning. Imagine what she might have done to that poor bridesmaid.

I love you, Phoebe, she thought.

She would be disappointed when she found out that she wasn't pregnant.

Allison used to love watching TV in a hotel room, but now it did not feel much different from watching TV in Danny Yang's Fort Lee apartment. His apartment was essentially a fancy hotel, but the swimming pool was closed.

The swimming pool was closed.

She had swum laps on the last day.

She had swum for an entire hour, not wanting it to be the last day at the pool, embarrassed for shedding tears when she was done. And then, the next day, she got on a flight to Miami, hoping that maybe it would be okay.

Allison did not want to believe that she would end her relationship with Danny because the swimming pool closed, but she felt as if she did not have a choice. She did not owe Danny anything. Or she owed him her life, but that didn't seem fair. It wasn't fair. It was too much pressure. Was she obligated to love him, be with him, spend her entire life in Fort Lee, New Jersey? She had been helpless, and he'd swooped in like a superhero.

There was nothing good on TV.

Allison went through all of the stations, once and then a second time. She stopped on an episode of *Star Trek*. The station must have been on a commercial the first time around.

Allison felt like it must be a sign.

There she was, in Miami, a place her father always wanted to go. Every winter he wanted to go to Miami, and she was in Miami. She had watched *Star Trek* with her father in his hospital room with him the night before he died. She would watch an episode of *Star Trek* for him now, in Miami. She wished that she could have brought his ashes, scattered them in the ocean.

Allison never thought she would watch this show again. She also never thought she would go back to that hospital. She never thought that she would be in a relationship with Danny Yang.

"Is that *Star Trek*?" Danny asked, his eyes still closed.

"It is," Allison said. "Do you like *Star Trek*?"

Danny nodded. "I do."

Allison had not known this. Somehow, it made her like him a little bit more. She did like him. He sat up on his pillows. He kissed Allison on her shoulder. It was such a small, nice thing to do. She could still change her mind about him.

She reserved that right. She did love him. The problem was, he was not the person she wanted to love.

She did not understand why he loved her. It seemed weird, unhealthy. She was not even pretty anymore. The camera-man had taken that, too, her hair, her faith in her looks. So then, looks, that wasn't it.

"This is a good one," Danny said. "Turn up the volume."

It was the same episode with Ashley Judd. The very one. The episode Allison had watched with her father in his hospital room the day he died.

"What a pretty girl," her father had said.

Now Allison watched the episode for the second time.

It had to mean something. Allison was not the kind of person to believe in anything, but this time, she did. Ashley Judd was such a pretty girl. Beautiful. Even in her funny spaceship uniform. It was so heartbreaking, really, just to look at her. One of Allison's favorite movies in the whole world was *Ruby in Paradise,* an indie film that almost no one remembered. In the movie, Ruby takes walks on the beach. She writes in her journal. She goes to a plant store and buys plants. Allison had been spellbound.

Harvey Weinstein had tried to ruin Ashley Judd's career, but he did not succeed. Instead, she changed course. Ashley Judd had become a public figure. She got her graduate degree, worked for the UN. She traveled to impoverished places and became the voice of millions of voiceless girls. After breaking her leg in the remotest region of the Congo, she gave an interview from her hospital bed, demonstrating how she had chewed on a stick to battle the pain when there was no pain medication. She was sharing her story, she said, in order to raise money so that women in the region could give birth on clean mats. Ashley Judd had become a force for good. Still. Allison wanted to take away all of the bad things that had ever happened to her.

"I hate what happened to her," Danny said when the episode was over.

"Me, too," Allison said.

Danny had no idea how he had just said exactly the right thing. "I am not a bad guy," Danny said.

"I don't think you are," Allison said.

"But you are thinking about leaving me."

Allison turned onto her side to face him. He turned onto his. They looked into each other's eyes.

"Don't leave me," he said, reaching for her hand. "Just because the swimming pool is closed."

"How did you know that?" Allison said.

"I know you," Danny said.

"You know the eighteen-year-old me," Allison said. "I'm not the same person."

"Neither am I," Danny said.

Really, Allison felt like she was the exact same person that she used to be.

"I don't really know who you are," Allison said.

"You do," Danny said. "We have spent the last month together," he said. "That is not an insignificant amount of time. I have loved this month."

Allison did not respond. She had loved swimming in the pool. She had loved ordering in food, eating with Danny, having sex with Danny, taking hot showers in his bathroom. But that was not her real life. Allison did not know what her real life was.

"You operated on my brain without asking me first,"

Allison said. "That was such a violation. And now we are together. It feels creepy. It feels wrong. Like you are taking advantage of me."

"Oh, Allison," Danny said. "I explained this to you. I didn't have a choice."

"I did not have a choice, either," Allison said slowly.

"You can choose now," Danny said.

Allison looked at him.

"I'm a good choice," he said. "I am no Harvey Weinstein."

Allison laughed.

"No, you're not," she said.

"Let's have hotel sex," Danny said. "What do you say? Order room service after."

"Do you want to?" Allison asked.

"Do you want to?" Danny asked.

"Not really," Allison said.

Normally that was exactly what Allison would want to do in a hotel room.

"Then let's not have sex," Danny said.

Danny kissed her.

It was a nice kiss.

He was a good kisser.

"I love you, Allison," Danny said.

"I love you, too," Allison said.

"This is real," Danny said. "You are not part of my imagination. Like some college fantasy. You are not a fantasy Allison."

"That's not even possible," Allison said with a laugh.

He touched the top of her head.

"Your hair feels soft," he said. "Like a baby duck's."

"I thought that, too."

Allison turned over onto her other side. Danny spooned her in his arms. Really, he was the same person he had been in college. She did know him. Danny was nice, and he loved her. This had always been true. This time, he did not have a long-distance girlfriend. This time, Allison was a little less starry-eyed. She had been out in the world. She did not particularly like it. For a long time, Allison had not felt safe, loved, looked out for, taken care of, respected. For a long time, Allison had not had a home. Maybe it was possible that Allison had loved her month in Fort Lee.

Maybe, this was her real life.

～～～～

Part
Six

*A*llison woke up early.

She felt something burning in her.

An unattended anger she could not let fester.

She left Danny Yang a note, writing it on hotel stationery. She would not be able to tell him to his face. She did not want it to be a text message. She had heard about people breaking up over text message. But she was not breaking up with him. It was just that there was something she had to do and Danny would not want her to go.

Allison packed her backpack and rode a blissfully empty elevator down to the lobby. She got a Cuban coffee and she sat on the beach, bare feet buried in the sand, watching the sun rise, drinking her coffee.

It was tempting to disappear, to find a place to stay in Miami, start a new kind of beach life. It would be easier, better, to stay with Danny, to catch the flight that night, to do all the things she was expected to do.

Visit her brother.

Get a proper job.

Open her mail.

Go to a gynecologist.

The life she was living was real. It was good, even.

But a voice in her head told her to go. To go now.

Those orange and white cats had been in her dreams again. The purring began at a lovely volume, and then got louder and louder, until the noise was worse than a vacuum cleaner, a leaf blower, a machine gun. Allison woke up, covered in sweat.

The dream was a message. Like the Ashley Judd episode of *Star Trek* was a message.

Allison did not know what it meant.

Save the cats? Save herself?

A part of Allison would have preferred to stay in bed with Danny. But she had no choice but to find out. It felt good to be alive. There were the pelicans on the beach. She was glad to be able to say goodbye.

"Goodbye, pelicans," she said.

She took a picture with her phone.

And then it was time to go.

〰〰

llison took a Lyft to a car-rental place. She rented a car. It was a red Acura. It was small, it was sporty. It was too sporty. It was not the kind of car Allison wanted to drive.

"Do you have something else?" she asked the woman who handed her the keys.

Allison knew that, statistically, red cars got pulled over more than other cars. This red car was practically a sports car. But this red car was what was available. Allison filled out the forms on the small screen on her phone because it was cheaper to get the car this way than to reserve the car on paper.

"Life is getting more and more surreal," Allison said to the woman behind the counter. She did not seem to have an opinion. She did not have pink hair. The car-rental woman did not deserve a greater place in Allison's story and, for that reason, Allison gazed at her a beat too long, knowing that soon she would be forgotten forever.

The second she walked out of the office she had already forgotten her.

"Hello, car," Allison said to the red car.

Allison was trusting her life to this car.

"Good car," she said.

Her brain, at least, was safely secured inside her head. She was safe to drive. It was 981 miles from Miami to her beach house in North Carolina. Where it used to be. It was an estimated driving time of fourteen hours, not including bathroom breaks and Starbucks coffee.

Allison also wanted to find Missy again. But Missy's Starbucks was above North Carolina, and Allison was currently below North Carolina. But maybe she could see Missy *after,* after North Carolina on her way back, her way back to Danny.

This drive was twice as long as the trip to New Jersey. But things, Allison told herself, were significantly better now.

She was, for instance, no longer dripping blood from a hole in her head.

Allison drove in the middle lane, above the speed limit, music playing on the radio. She had an extra cell phone charger. She had her health.

〰〰〰

*T*hree miles away from her destination, Allison made a detour, pulling into a Walmart. She had not gone to the Walmart in the brief time that she lived in her North Carolina beach house, but she thought it would be the right place for her at this moment in time.

Allison got an enormous shopping cart and wandered up and down the aisles, taking her time. She was not entirely sure what she wanted. She only knew that she wanted a lot of things. Not sure where she would sleep that night, Allison picked out an easy-to-assemble two-person tent. She bought a sleeping bag. A pillow. A pillowcase. She put cheese puffs into her cart and several bars of dark chocolate with salted caramel. A bag of Honeycrisp apples. A six-pack of stemless plastic champagne flutes. Somehow, she needed them. Allison did not know such a thing existed.

She got two bottles of Italian mineral water. A tall glass vase. And then, after a moment's hesitation, a second one.

Allison got a bag of dry cat food. Metal bowls for the cat food. The water.

Earplugs. A pregnancy test.

She did not need all of these things.

Just in case.

She could donate the cat food to an animal shelter.

The cats did not need to be rescued.

She was out of pens.

In the stationery aisle, Allison found a package of black gel pens. They were good pens, her favorite Japanese brand, and she was pleased to find them in a Walmart. She picked out a bunch of tulips, too, that were at the cash register.

The tulips were pretty. Purple.

It had been years since she had been in a Walmart. The store was just as ugly as she remembered it, but it was also significantly better. She did not know when the store had begun to carry such quality items. Allison was pleased with all of her purchases.

As she took her items out of the cart, her cell phone started to ring. Allison could not not look. It was Danny. Allison let it ring. She had several unread text messages from him, too.

It felt wrong not to answer these calls, not to talk to him. Allison did not know if she was doing the right thing, but she was doing it. She had to.

Allison also knew that he would be distressed if he knew where she was.

If he knew her plan.

He would tell her to stop. He might call the police.

She was being kind, really, saving him from worry.

"I'm sorry, Danny," Allison said.

He would understand.

The cashier looked at her.

"Do you ever think out loud?" Allison said.

This cashier was no Missy.

It was possible she was the same woman from the car-rental place, with a different hairstyle.

"I have a hole in my head," Allison said, pointing to the

almost bald spot on her head. The hole had sealed, but to Allison, it would always be there.

"That sucks," the cashier said.

Allison was pleased. The cashier had given her a suitable answer.

"It does," Allison said. "I did nothing to deserve it."

"No one deserves that," the cashier said.

Allison smiled at her.

The cashier looked confused. She started to bag Allison's items. Allison paid for her purchases and loaded them into her red car. She would talk to Danny later, when she was done. She would talk to him soon.

Allison was tired. Exhausted. She had driven for a long time. She still had things to do. Allison ate a Honeycrisp apple in the parking lot, sitting in her red car. She made sure to put her seat belt on before she started the ignition.

〰〰〰

Allison stared at what was left of her little blue house.

The front two steps leading up to a porch, and a house, that were no longer there.

The red couch was still there, pools of rainwater collecting in the cushions. A ceramic toilet in the grass where the bathroom used to be. It looked like a photograph. The sun was setting and the sky was a stunning pink and purple. There was yellow police tape surrounding the perimeter of what used to be a building.

CAUTION.

Keep out.

This was still her property.

The grass had grown long. She had not mowed it in the week and a half that she had lived there. She was surprised by how lovely it looked now, overgrown and wild. There were yellow and pink wildflowers. It was beautiful. If Allison lived here, she would want to keep the lawn like this.

Allison owned this beautiful mess.

Someone had suggested to her that she could rebuild. She could not remember who. Maybe it was her brother. Her friend Lori. She had not talked to Lori again since that one strange, sad visit to Fort Lee. It could have been Danny, but that seemed unlikely. Because he would not want her to live in North Carolina. Most likely it was her mother. A part of a conversation that she only half listened to, along with the part about the hospital bills, which she was pretty sure she had paid.

But, much as Allison liked the wildflowers, much as she loved the ocean and the way the air felt, she would not rebuild this house. This place was done for her.

Allison climbed over the yellow plastic caution tape and sat down on her front step. She had a moment's worry that it was not steady. But, really, how far was there left to fall.

Allison closed her eyes.

For a very short time, Allison had been happy here.

She was tired.

She had driven all day.

She could stay here.

She had a tent.

The sun was starting to set and the sky would turn to black. She would get up, put up the tent, maybe near the broken toilet. She could pee in the toilet. All she had to do was get up, get up and get the tent from the sporty red car parked in the driveway. It was her driveway. Which seemed funny. Allison was glad that she could still amuse herself. *Soon*, Allison thought. She did not open her eyes. She wished she had made love with Danny the night before. Or early in the morning. He could have fallen back asleep after. Allison opened her eyes. Closed them again.

She woke up with a start to a different sky.

It was full of stars.

There weren't stars like this in Fort Lee, New Jersey.

Allison had not meant to fall asleep, sitting up on the

front step. Awake again, she forced herself to get up. She went to her red car and opened the trunk. She took out her Walmart tent. The poles were already attached to the fabric. It pretty much was an instant tent, as advertised on the packaging. This was a relief for Allison. She had never gone camping as a child. This could change, though. Allison could become a person who liked to camp.

Allison could take Phoebe camping.

They could go camping with Danny.

They would be like one of those beautiful biracial families that were becoming so popular on TV shows and clothing catalogs. She had not, of course, told Danny about the idea of Phoebe. The possibility of Phoebe. Allison still had to wrap her head around the idea of Danny. Add to it happily ever after. The nuclear family.

Why not her?

What was so wrong with that?

Allison had never been a rebel. She just lived her life, day to day, each day wondering how to get through that particular day.

Allison had a purpose now: getting ready for bed. She got out of her tent, went back to the car again, and got out her new sleeping bag. She also took out a bottle of mineral water. The cheese puffs. She put these things down on the orange plastic floor of her tent, but she did not climb inside.

She had to go to the bathroom.

She stepped carefully over the yellow tape again, back into the space that had once been her house. She pulled up her gray silk dress and peed into the toilet.

It made her laugh. The pee was going, essentially, straight to the ground. At least it did not run down her legs. She had not remembered to buy toilet paper. Allison saw a light go on in the house next door. A man's face looking out the window, looking down at her, watching her pee. Allison's heart started to race. She had not liked her neighbor. And her neighbor, she realized, had not liked her, either. Still, there was no reason to be afraid.

Allison pulled up her underwear. She stood up from the toilet, hoping that she could air-dry her private parts and not get her new dress too dirty. She probably was not supposed to pee in this toilet, though it had never occurred to her not to. The idea was so funny.

She looked down at her pee, some of it still floating in the bowl. It was very yellow. She must be dehydrated. She would drink more water, moving on. She reached to flush the toilet, but realized how silly that would be.

She told herself to stay calm.

She went back to her tent and got her bottle of mineral water.

She took a long drink.

Allison was not surprised to see the neighbor from next door emerge from his brick house. He really was the big pig. She was surprised to see that he was carrying a hunting rifle. That seemed a little bit over the top.

At least to her. Allison was not a threat.

She could not say the same about him.

For the life of her, Allison could not remember this man's name.

"What do you think you are doing?" he said, walking across his lawn and onto hers. "You're trespassing."

Really, he was the trespasser. He was also pointing the gun at Allison.

This was a new experience. Allison did not like it. Allison put her hand on her stomach. She thought of all the Black men—boys, sometimes—who were shot for doing so much less. She was white. She was wearing a dress.

"Actually, I think you are the one trespassing," Allison said. "This was my house. This is my property. We've met before. I'm Allison."

Allison looked down at her hands. They were trembling.

She remembered the man's name.

"You're Jim," she said. "Tough luck," she said. "That is what you told me. After the hurricane. You know me."

"You look different," he said, gun still cocked.

"I cut my hair," Allison said.

"You ain't planning on camping here, are you?" he asked.

He still hadn't lowered the gun.

"I was thinking about it," Allison said. "Just for tonight. But I don't have to. I mean I won't. I won't camp here."

"It's not that kind of neighborhood," Jim said.

"It's not?" Allison asked.

"No," he said. "It's not."

"Okay," Allison said. "That's fine."

Allison thought that it was legal to set up a tent on your own land. She remembered when she was a kid, how she and her friends used to set up a tent in the backyard for sleepovers.

"I could have you arrested for peeing on the lawn."

Allison did not respond. She did not know if that was true.

"This place looks like a trash heap," Jim said. "I've already called the sheriff. It's an eyesore, bringing down property values. For all I know, there is a warrant out for your arrest."

Allison stared at his very big gun. He still had not lowered it.

This—the neighbor, the gun—had not been part of her plan. She had wanted to go back to her house. Acknowledge that it had existed. Acknowledge what had happened to her. Make sure it had all been real.

Not this.

She took a deep breath in. She thought about Danny. She could be on an airplane with him, maybe right now, eating Peanut M&M's and leaning her head on his shoulder. Now he would be sitting alone on the plane.

"I'll buy this land off you," Jim said. "I'll clear up the mess. Take all that hassle off of your hands."

"That would be nice," Allison said.

It actually would be. Allison did not want to deal with the hassle. She also knew, even while being held at gunpoint, how much this pig wanted this land. It would expand his property, increase the value of his brick house. He was not doing her any favors. It made her not want to sell. Later, not threatened at gunpoint, Allison would sit in front of her computer and research the property values. She would ask for more than it was worth. She would turn a profit on her lost beach house. Her broken dreams. She remembered, then, the story of the realtor who didn't like him. He had volunteered this information. He had called her a cunt.

"I'll give you a good price," Jim said. "You can trust me."

"I am always inclined to trust a man pointing a gun at me," Allison said.

She was not sure it was a smart time to make a joke.

Allison looked past Jim at her Walmart tent. She was more tired than sad. Than scared. She would not be able to sleep in this tent. It had seemed cozy inside, nice. She thought about the cheese puffs that she did not get to eat.

Allison asked Jim for his cell phone number, as if this were a normal conversation to be having with your next-door neighbor while being held at gunpoint. It was crazy how he did not put the gun down. Maybe he thought this intimidated her.

It did. But she would not negotiate that night.

She entered his number into her phone.

"Got it," she said. "I'll be in touch," she said. "You can talk to my realtor."

She would get that realtor, the one who did not like him.

Trying hard not to shake, Allison slowly walked away. She got into the red car, leaving the tent and the sleeping bag and the unopened bag of cheese puffs behind.

Walmart purchases.

Nothing more.

~~~~~

Allison had lost faith in her plan.

It would be smarter to give up and drive back to Danny. She no longer had the swimming pool, but he did have a nice, clean bathtub. Good water pressure. That stack of menus. She could keep on driving; she could be at that rest-stop Starbucks in a matter of hours. A coffee and a croissant. She did not have to do anything that made her feel afraid.

But, she told herself, the trip to her old house had been a success.

She was, for instance, not dead.

She was going to sell her property for a profit. She was sure that would happen. She had come this far. Allison decided to stick to her plan, and her plan was to drive to the cameraman's house.

~~~~~

llison stared at the house. Where it had happened. Allison should have recognized it, but she didn't. This was where Google Search said that he lived. There was no van in the driveway. No fancy bicycle. No yellow marigolds like in the picture on the Internet.

"After this, I'm coming home," Allison said to herself, but really talking to Danny, who, of course, could not hear her.

She still had not told him where she was because she knew he would tell her to leave, that she had nothing to prove, and that was true, but it also wasn't. She needed to do this first.

"After this," she said.

The cameraman's house was like the checkout woman at the car rental. Allison tried, but she could no longer see that woman's face. It could be the wrong house. But Allison did have faith in Google. Google said she had arrived. That motherfucking cameraman had stolen something from her, and she wanted it back. She only had to figure out what it was.

She could not get bludgeoned twice. Odds, at least, were against it.

Allison carefully stepped out of the car.

Allison could almost see herself move, as if this were a scene from a movie. The audience would be screaming at the screen. *No! Don't do it. Don't go in the house.*

Maybe, someday, she would write it all down.

Another script.

Maybe that was why she was still wearing her gray silk dress. Not just because it was comfortable, but because it would look good on a screen. But, really, it was probably because of how much Allison loved this dress. She wished she had bought two of them. Three.

Her cell phone started to ring.

It was, of course, a bad time for her phone to ring.

She did not want to announce her arrival.

Allison took the phone from her pocket and declined the call as fast as she could. Danny Yang.

Poor Danny.

He just had to wait a little bit longer.

"I promise," Allison said.

They did not have that kind of relationship. He could not hear her voice from hundreds of miles away. She had left that note saying that she would be home soon, but he had no reason to trust her. Allison stood outside the house. She was being cautious. She was being smart. She was smart. She waited for a light to turn on. It stayed dark.

It was better, of course, that the cameraman was not there.

Allison walked up to the front door and then stepped onto the lawn. She looked into the living room window. There was one light on, a floor lamp. Allison saw an orange and white cat asleep on an armchair. And there was the other one, asleep on the couch. The cats. She had dreamed about these cats.

They were real. This was the right house.

She had not imagined what had happened to her.

Allison pressed her hands against the glass.

The police officer had told her that the cameraman had checked himself in to a mental hospital. How long ago had that been? How long would the cameraman stay in the mental hospital?

Allison had not pressed charges. Had that been a mistake? He could leave that hospital and return home, find her there. But she would not stay long. She would not stay. Really, she just wanted to pet the cats.

She tried the front door of the house and it was locked.

There was a large flowerpot in front of the door and Allison lifted it and found a key. It was too easy.

Allison picked up the key and she put it into the lock and the key turned and she walked inside the house.

"What the fuck are you doing, Allison?" Allison asked herself.

Her plan had been to drive to the house and look at it. She had done that. She had had ideas, maybe, of what could happen next, but had not thought it through.

In a movie, would the young woman entering the house where she had once been assaulted talk to herself? Allison did not know. She had not written the script.

It did not make sense that she was talking, out loud, announcing herself. But if the cameraman *was* in the house, wasn't it better that she announce herself? She did not, for instance, want to get shot. This was something homeowners often did to intruders. Unlike the man in the brick house, the cameraman would not have a gun.

What the cameraman did have was a glass vase. But he had broken it already. On top of her head. She was safe.

I am safe, Allison told herself.

She had every right to be there.

She remembered this room. The couch. The armchair. The cats.

Allison touched the hole in her head.

It was still closed.

Okay, Allison told herself. *Still safe.*

Allison took two steps backward, out of the house, and went back to the car. She rifled through her Walmart bags in the backseat.

She grabbed one of the glass vases.

She noticed the tulips and knew that she should put them in water, but she was not going to do that. That was too much to ask of herself. She had bought them at the Walmart, she realized, in order not to seem suspicious. Which was funny, in a way. Buying vases, in itself, was not a suspicious act.

Allison could only do what she could do.

She went back inside the cameraman's house. She sat on the couch next to the big cat and she petted it. "Good cat," she said.

The cat purred.

Allison put the glass vase on a cushion next to her. She felt better knowing it was there.

~~~~~

Allison closed her eyes, petting the cat.

The cat was so soft. She had missed him.

She had come back for him.

She had never had a cat before.

She used to believe that she was not responsible enough to have a pet.

〰〰

llison had fallen asleep, sitting up.

Again.

She was still on the cameraman's couch.

She reached up and gently touched the hole in her head. Still closed.

The cat on the couch was no longer on the couch.

Allison reached into her pocket for her cell phone. It wasn't fully charged anymore but was still at seventy percent. Still good. She had to pee. It was problematic, how often she needed to pee.

Allison told herself that she wasn't scared, but she was also aware of the fact that her heart was racing. For a moment, she had forgotten how she had gotten back into the cameraman's house. That she had driven there, entered entirely on her own volition. It was her idea. She looked at her phone. Two hours had passed. It was the middle of the night. There was another text message from Danny.

Please call me and let me know that you are okay. Please.

"Hello?" she called out.

No answer.

She was still alone in the house.

She had a glass vase, still on the couch, at her side, to protect herself with if necessary.

Allison would not call Danny, but she thought about calling Lori. She needed someone to support her. Or tell her to stop this nonsense. Probably, Lori would tell Allison that she was a fucking idiot.

Lori would tell Allison to run. To run. Leave. Get the fuck out. Lori could not always be relied upon, but she would do that for Allison.

It was the only sensible thing to do.

Run.

But Allison really had to pee.

And so, she went to the bathroom.

Allison remembered where it was, the bathroom. Her bathroom. The guest bathroom. Allison made it to the toilet in time.

She peed.

She washed her hands.

She looked at herself in the mirror. She could see herself: the short hair, the gray dress. But she could see the other Allison, that woman with the green skin, bloodshot eyes, blood dripping from her forehead, clotted in her long hair. Allison missed her hair.

Allison had thrown up in this sink.

Remembering this made Allison feel like she might throw up again. She sat down on the bathroom floor.

Please, she thought, a silent prayer.

She did not want to throw up.

In Allison's mind, there really was almost nothing worse than throwing up. And there was no reason to throw up. She had not been hit on the head with a vase. She had no food in her stomach. She had eaten only an apple. A Walmart apple. And that was hours ago. But her head had started to throb, pain radiating from where the hole in her head used to be.

This, she realized with complete certainty, had been a mistake. A big mistake. An enormous mistake. She needed to run, to get the fuck out of there, but instead, she was sitting on the bathroom floor, hugging her knees.

I can get out of this, she told herself. *I can do this.*

Allison knew that was what she had to do. Stand up, get out of the bathroom. Find a cat, preferably the bigger one.

Go.

Do not delay.

But the throbbing in her head had gotten worse. She could not believe how much her head hurt.

Allison leaned over and threw up into the toilet.

There. She had done it. She had thrown up. She was so mad at herself. So unbelievably mad. This did not have to be her life. She had done this to herself. She had driven to this house, let herself in. She was a moron.

Allison threw up again.

She thought she would die.

And then, she felt better.

Phoebe, she thought.

A revelation. Maybe this was Phoebe talking to her. Maybe, maybe, this was morning sickness. Allison had forgotten all about Phoebe. She had bought a pregnancy test at the Walmart. It was in the red car.

Allison touched her flat stomach. Maybe she had lost her mind. Somehow, she had not vomited on her dress. This seemed like a good thing.

Allison stood up and went into the guest bedroom. She had to sleep. She did not have a choice. It seemed crazy, to be back in this house, to go to sleep in this bed. It had been real. The cameraman, the glass vase. This room. The cats. This house. Sometimes, it felt as if she had made it all up.

But there was the white comforter on the bed. It was clean. No bloodstains. How was that possible? There was no sign that she had ever been there. Both of the cats were on the bed, curled up next to each other.

Allison lay down. She did not see another way. She could barely keep her eyes open. There was no one in the house. Just the cats. The cats were good cats. They seemed to like her, and she liked them.

Allison got under the covers. The sheets were clean, too. Someone must have come into the house, taken off the ruined bedding, made the bed. But the house was empty now. She was safe.

"We are safe," Allison told Phoebe. "Don't worry."

The last thing she saw before she fell asleep was her water bottle. It was on the floor in the corner of the room. Her favorite water bottle with the little pink flowers. She had thought she had lost it forever, but this was where it had been. All this time.

This was the missing piece of her life, and she had gotten it back.

〰〰〰

llison woke up with the sun.

The pain in her head was gone.

The nausea was gone.

The cats were gone.

Allison touched her head. No blood. The hole still closed. She had survived this strange experiment. She had had something to prove to herself and she had proven it.

Allison got out of the bed.

She was still wearing her gray silk dress. Her wedding dress. This made her smile. It was the dress she wore to the wedding. Maybe she would marry Danny Yang. She could wear this dress, but maybe a new one. Clean. A dress she had never vomited in. Allison picked up her water bottle. She loved this water bottle. She walked with the bottle into the living room, holding it to her chest.

An orange and white cat slept on the couch, in the same place as the night before. This was the bigger one, lying right next to her glass vase. The other cat was sleeping on the armchair. These must be their favorite places. The cats slowly opened their eyes, as if to acknowledge Allison, and then closed them again. Allison wondered if the cats were lonely, all alone in the cameraman's house. Someone must come to feed them. Allison had to leave. It was crazy that she was still here.

She had slept surprisingly well.

She would tell Danny this story when she went home. How scared she had been. For no reason.

And then she noticed something. There on the round table, Allison noticed the other Walmart flower vase, and in the vase, the purple tulips that she had left in the backseat of the car. In the kitchen, Allison could see a fresh pot of coffee in the coffeemaker.

The cameraman stepped into the living room.

"You're awake," he said with a smile.

Allison did not know what to say. She did not have words.

She set her water bottle down on the couch and picked up the vase.

"Hurricane Girl," he said. "It's so nice to see you again."

He had poured her a cup of coffee.

"You take half-and-half?" he asked.

Allison nodded.

She watched as the cameraman went back into the kitchen and poured cream into her coffee.

Allison could not have been more stupid. She understood this. But she was not afraid. She felt clear-eyed, full of purpose. She wanted to kill him. She wanted to hurt him badly, the way he had hurt her.

Her hands, she noticed, were shaking.

The throbbing in her head had begun again.

"I like your hair," he said. "You cut it short."

"Thank you," Allison said.

The cameraman walked over to Allison, handing her the cup of coffee. Allison was not sure what she was going to do. She took a sip of the coffee. She wanted this coffee. And like the last time, the coffee was good. This, she realized, was her do-over.

It was perfect.

"You read my note?" the cameraman said. "Is that why you are here? I am back on my medication. I'm not a violent person. I had been off my meds. I'm so sorry," he said. "I'm so happy you are back. I will make it up to you. You could live here, with me. We could be so happy."

Allison stared at him.

"Sit down," he said, motioning to a chair at the round table. "You look pale. Are you hungry? Do you want breakfast?"

Allison shook her head. She did not sit down.

"I have raspberries," he said. "Yogurt. What you had the last time? I could make you a waffle? Tell me. Whatever you want. I will make it for you. If I don't have it, I will buy it for you."

"No," Allison said. "I'm not hungry."

Allison took another sip of coffee.

Allison ignored the throbbing of her head.

She walked over to the round table, standing next to the cameraman. She put her mug of coffee on the table. She was taller than him. The cameraman. Keith. She had known better, as soon as he told her his name. He was exactly like she'd remembered him. Small. Balding. Wire-framed glasses. He was wearing the same pair of cargo shorts. He had large knees, skinny legs.

He was nothing. He was nobody. Allison put her hand on the back of his head, and the cameraman tilted his head up toward her, to be kissed, and she reached over and brought the glass vase down on top of his head.

Pieces of glass cascaded around the cameraman.

Small chips, like green diamonds.

Blood began to pour down the cameraman's forehead.

One of the cats meowed.

Allison touched her stomach.

Phoebe. She hoped Phoebe had not seen this.

Allison picked up the mug of coffee from the table and took one last sip. She felt surprisingly calm. This was, in fact, much better than last time. She was doing it right. She looked at the cameraman, whose eyes were open wide. Blood was streaming over his eyes. He had begun to blink furiously. He opened his mouth to speak and began to gasp instead. "Help me," he pleaded. "Help me."

Allison patted the pocket of her gray dress. She had her cell phone. She had her car keys.

Allison scooped up the cat from the couch. It was the big one. She could hear him purr. "Kitty," she said. She hoped that Phoebe would like this cat. She hoped that Danny was not allergic to cats. She could not remember. She was keeping the cat. The other cat looked at her, his tail flickering back and forth.

"You can come, too," she said.

The cat did not move.

Allison picked up her flowered water bottle with her free hand. She took a long, deep breath. She opened the front door to the cameraman's house and she did not look back.

The sun was shining.

The sky was blue.

It was a beautiful day.

~~~~~

ACKNOWLEDGMENTS

Hurricane Girl is my fifth novel, and sometimes I cannot believe it. I am grateful to Knopf for publishing this book and doing such a beautiful job. My editor Jenny Jackson is a joy to work with. As are Maris Dyer and Reagan Arthur and the entire team working behind the scenes. I am grateful to my agent Alex Glass, who championed this book from the start. I am grateful to Shelley Salamensky for always wanting to read new pages and reading them right away. To my family who continues to love me even if I have a way of making that tricky. Thank you, Julie Dermansky, for suggesting that I write a scene about karma that time when I was feeling stuck. To my friends, who sometimes don't even know when they are along for the ride: Sarah Bardin, Allison Radecki, Robin Romm, Lizzie Skurnick, Lynn Steger Strong, Sondra Wolfer, and Kevin Wilson. And to my daughter Nina and the cats who give me a reason to do what I do.

A NOTE ABOUT THE AUTHOR

Marcy Dermansky is the author of the critically acclaimed novels *Very Nice, The Red Car, Bad Marie,* and *Twins.* She has received fellowships from MacDowell and the Edward F. Albee Foundation. She lives with her daughter in Montclair, New Jersey.

marcydermansky.com
Twitter and Instagram @mdermansky

A NOTE ON THE TYPE

This book was set in Legacy Serif. Ronald Arnholm (b. 1939) designed the Legacy family after being inspired by the 1470 edition of *Eusebius* set in the roman type of Nicolas Jenson. This revival type maintains much of the character of the original. Its serifs, stroke weights, and varying curves give Legacy Serif its distinct appearance. It was released by the International Typeface Corporation in 1992.

Typeset by Scribe,
Philadelphia, Pennsylvania

Printed and bound by Berryville Graphics,
Berryville, Virginia